FEAR THE FALLOUT

NUCLEAR DAWN BOOK TWO

KYLA STONE

PAPER MOON PRESS

Fear the Fallout

Printed in the United States of America

Cover design by Christian Bentulan

Book formatting by Vellum

First Printed in 2019

ISBN: 978-1-945410-30-7

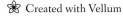 Created with Vellum

To Jeremy, for holding down the fort while I made up imaginary people in imaginary worlds.

PROLOGUE

ZERO HOUR MINUS THIRTY-FOUR MINUTES...

Thirty minutes before the first bomb detonated, a sea-green Honda Odyssey pulled up to the curb in front of the Smithsonian National Museum in Washington, D.C., just a few blocks from the Capitol Building and the White House.

A fading stick-figure family sticker peeled from the rear lefthand window. A bulging diaper bag sat on the floor amid wadded Taco Bell wrappers and a sippy cup.

A bulky cardboard box took up the entire rear of the vehicle, the kind that might house a compact fridge or shiny new front-loading washing machine. The mid and rear windows were tinted black.

No one bothered to give the minivan anything beyond a cursory glance. It looked like a thousand family minivans they'd seen before.

Even the man who exited the vehicle—a middle-aged guy wearing jeans and a wrinkled Star Wars T-shirt, a Washington Redskins cap shoved low over his forehead—aroused no suspicion.

After he paid the parking meter, the man strolled along the sidewalk, diaper bag over one shoulder, a selfie-stick in one hand.

Just another tourist enjoying the fine, sunny day in the bustling Capitol of the United States of America.

No one noticed the second car—dark blue Ford Taurus, nondescript—slide up next to him and open the door as he slipped inside. The car pulled into traffic and drove away, just under the speed limit, toward the Anacostia River.

The man in the Redskins cap shifted in the passenger seat of the Ford Taurus and checked the GPS. He punched in a saved number on a pre-paid, disposable phone.

"The time was moved up," said the deep voice on the other end. "Did you receive the message?"

"We did. We're in position," said the passenger. "Everything is ready."

The man on the other end grunted in approval.

"There is a time for everything under the sun," the passenger said as he pulled a small device from his pocket.

"God be with us," said the other man.

The driver said nothing. He did not honk at a jaywalking pedestrian as he pulled onto a less congested side street and parked in Giesboro Park off MacDill Blvd, almost six miles from Capitol Hill.

With one hand still on the wheel, he pulled a specialized pair of sunglasses over his eyes. The passenger did the same. He glanced at the clock on the dashboard. 12:37 p.m.

"The judgment begins," he said.

The man pressed the button of the device he held in his hand.

A hundredth of a second later, the bomb exploded.

In the instant of detonation, the core of the bomb scorched a blistering 300,000 degrees Celsius, fifty times hotter than the surface of the sun itself.

In less than a second, tens of thousands of people were cremated, instantly carbonized into charred, smoking ash. They were vaporized where they slept, stood, walked, sat, drove—simply gone.

The intensity of the thermal blast ignited birds in midair. Clothing, trees, dogs and cats, and cars spontaneously combusted. Steel liquefied, melting like wax.

The fireball shot above the city, expanding as it rose until it blotted out everything in a great flash of extraordinary brilliance.

It was as if the sun had fallen to earth.

After the flash came a deafening boom. And then the shockwave, a towering wall of tremendous pressure slamming through Capitol Hill, crushing monuments and museums: the Smithsonian, the Capitol building, the Library of Congress, the Supreme Court building, the Washington Monument, the White House.

Six miles from ground zero, the Ford Taurus pulled away from the park and entered traffic already pouring out of the city. There was still room to maneuver around the crashed vehicles and escape, though there wouldn't be for long.

As the Taurus fled the city, the passenger twisted in his seat, staring back at the broiling, radioactive mushroom cloud swelling above Washington D.C.—not in horror, but with an awestruck thrill of vindication.

It was only the third time in history a nuclear bomb had ever been used against civilians.

It wouldn't be the last.

1

DAKOTA

ZERO HOUR PLUS FIFTY HOURS...

The sky over Miami was a dour, sullen gray-brown. In the distance, smoke rose in hazy columns over the shopping plaza rooftop.

Nineteen-year-old Dakota Sloane suppressed a shudder. She hated fire.

Dread tightened in her chest like a closed fist. She'd felt the same sense of foreboding before each foster or group home placement.

And she'd felt it often during her years at the compound—each time she was compelled to the mercy room, where the only mercy she'd ever received was the relief of unconsciousness.

Her skin prickled at the memory. Phantom pain radiated from the old burns across her back with a throbbing heat. She couldn't see the scars, but not for a single instant did she ever forget they were there.

"Dakota?" Julio de la Peña, the middle-aged Cuban bartender, asked. He stood in the shattered doorway of the Walgreens and raked his hands through his graying black hair. "You okay?"

Two days ago, a nuclear bomb had exploded in downtown

Miami, only moments after similar bombs detonated in New York City and Washington, D.C. Dakota and her companions had been lucky to escape with their lives.

Now, after two days holed up in a theater to avoid the worst of the radioactive fallout, they were venturing out into the city to rescue Dakota's sister, Eden, and get the hell out of the hot zone.

Dakota lifted her chin. You faced the future with courage or cowardice; it was coming for you either way. *Just breathe.* "Ready."

She pointed at the fine layer of grit filming the shopping plaza parking lot ahead of them, toward the vehicles, shopping carts, and palm trees. "Most of the fallout in the air is gone, but we still need to worry about radiation contamination from groundshine."

"What's that, now?" Julio asked.

"After the radioactive particles descend from the mushroom cloud, they land on the ground and mix with dirt and dust," Dakota said. "Not just the ground, but on the surface of everything. Remember, radiation is invisible. You can't see or feel it."

"In other words, don't touch anything," said Logan Garcia.

"Pretty much." She pointed toward a road at the west end of the parking lot. "This way."

Though it felt like a lifetime ago and a world away, they were still only five blocks from the Beer Shack on Front Street, a few miles from downtown Miami. Just in case they ever needed to run, she'd memorized the various routes to Eden's house from both the bar and her apartment.

"We can take 9th Street north toward Wynwood for almost a mile and a half, then west a half mile, until we hit Bay Point Drive. Another half mile, then it's a couple of small side streets to Palm Cove. My sister lives off of Bellview Court."

"Palm Cove, huh?" Logan cocked his brows. "Nice digs."

Julio was looking at her strangely, his forehead furrowed.

She knew he was wondering about her insistence on being paid cash under the table, the mile-long walk she made to and from work to avoid bus and taxi fares. Her cheap Goodwill clothes. Her lack of credit cards, bank accounts, or a driver's license.

Now here was her sister, holed up in a fancy gated community where every house featured a kidney-shaped pool with a spa and automated waterfall, their manicured lawns perfectly green even in winter, with maids and landscapers to care for it all.

"It's a long story," she muttered.

She didn't owe them an explanation. It wasn't any of their business.

Not even Julio knew she'd been a foster kid. And no one but Ezra Burrows knew where she and Eden had come from.

It was too dangerous.

She adjusted the shoulder bag and the strap of the M4 and strode into the parking lot, winding between dozens of stalled and abandoned cars as the others followed her in silence.

She took the lead, Logan at her side, Julio helping Shay hobble along just behind them. Shay would slow them down, but some things couldn't be helped.

Even adjusted for the slower pace, they should still make it to Eden and escape the hot zone in time.

She forced herself to focus on taking in their surroundings. In every building—storefronts, apartments and condos, office suites—the windows and doors gaped like broken-toothed mouths.

Shattered glass and debris littered the ground. Portions of some walls and ceilings had collapsed, but most were still standing.

The sidewalks were too dangerous, so they walked along the middle of the street, weaving between the husks of cars, SUVs, trucks, and buses.

Hundreds of vehicles cluttered the roads. Several were crushed or overturned from accidents, but some suffered only dented fenders or hoods.

Still others remained in pristine condition, their flung-open doors the only sign that something had happened, that their inhabitants had fled for their lives.

As far as they could see, nothing moved anywhere: no people, no birds or squirrels. Nothing living.

"Where are all the people?" Julio whispered.

"Those not too injured by the blast, flying debris, and car accidents must have walked out," Dakota said.

"Even for those people exposed to high levels of radiation, the symptoms won't manifest for several days or weeks," Shay Harris said. "Except in the worst cases, like the man in the theater."

Shay winced and touched the bandage wrapped around her head. Less than an hour ago, she'd been shot by the first survivor they'd met, a Blood Outlaw gangster defending his newly stolen turf. Luckily, the bullet had only grazed her skull.

Even luckier, Shay was a third-year nursing student who had talked Dakota through her medical care. Sweat beaded her brown skin. Her thick, springy coils were matted with dried blood. But she was on her feet, albeit with Julio's help.

"If they can get medical care in time, most of them will make it," Shay said with forced brightness.

Dakota had her doubts, but she kept them to herself.

They lapsed into a strained silence.

As they walked, she studied Logan out of the corner of her eye. He was tall, lean, and muscular. A few of his tattoos peeked out beneath his new long-sleeved shirt. Though he was only in his mid-twenties, he already had a tough, weathered look to him, his dark eyes hard and alert—when he wasn't drunk.

He stared straight ahead. She couldn't read his expression beneath the scarf covering the lower half of his face, but she didn't really care. She was still furious at him.

The idiot gangbanger had swung the M4 in the air like a toy, giving Logan his opening. A bullet to the brain would've dropped the thug like a rock.

The scumbag would be dead; Shay would be fine. And without a distraction, the second gangbanger wouldn't have escaped to give their descriptions to his gangster boss.

All because Logan hesitated.

And for what?

He wasn't a soldier after all. Then what was he, besides a liar, a drunk, and an ex-con? And what had he done hard time for?

Did it really matter? Everyone had skeletons in their closet, baggage they didn't want anyone else to know about. She had her own secrets to hide.

But her secrets wouldn't endanger the group. She had a dark, uneasy feeling that Logan's secrets would.

What about Maddox? a voice niggled at the back of her mind. She pushed it away. If she warned them about Maddox, she'd have to tell them the whole sordid story, and that she couldn't bring herself to do.

The shame and the fear were buried too deep. Even the thought of someone knowing filled her with a rush of hollow terror.

If Maddox appeared, she could just tell Logan he was a gangster and have him shot before he could get a word out. Or maybe she'd pull the Glock from Logan's holster and do it herself. That was the better play.

Either way, she had the situation under control.

She hated depending on anyone but herself. Everyone in her entire life had only let her down. Her parents had abandoned her in death. Her Aunt Ada had refused to protect her from the punishments meted out at the compound.

Maddox had made her a hundred promises she'd been naïve enough to believe.

Then there were the indifferent foster parents and group home leaders, either cruel, incompetent, or simply too overwhelmed to notice the terrible things happening beneath their noses.

Only Ezra had never let her down.

Dakota was the one who'd abandoned him.

Depending on anyone but herself left her open and vulnerable. She despised that sickening, out-of-control feeling, that panicky tightening of her chest.

She gripped the M4. She'd give her right arm to have a few magazines full of 5.56 mm caliber rounds right now.

The world had still gone to hell, but at least she'd have some semblance of control.

But the M4 was empty. All she had was her tactical knife. And the only one with a loaded gun was also half-drunk.

At least now she knew not to trust him as far as she could throw him. But she still needed to get the truth out of him and assess the level of danger he posed to the group in general and her goals in particular.

The sooner she rid herself of him, the better. She cursed herself for not just stealing his pistol back at the theater and leaving them all behind.

That would've been the smarter move.

But it was too late, now. All she could do was figure out what to do going forward.

In her head, she ticked off the new plan: rescue her sister; get Shay to a hospital outside the hot zone; head west to the Tamiami Trail without being accosted by Maddox or any other desperate souls; lose Logan; make it to the cabin with Eden.

That was it. She had no thought beyond immediate safety.

Once they were at Ezra's where they belonged, she'd create a new plan—one for their future.

Dakota stopped suddenly. Her entire body stiffened. "What is that?"

2

LOGAN

Logan Garcia already regretted his decision to leave the theater.

The sweltering heat was nearly intolerable. His sweat-damp clothes clung to his body, and the scorched air felt like it was choking him, cutting off his breath.

That all-too-familiar thirst burned in his throat, buzzed in his head.

The world was too real, too harsh.

He was far too sober. He needed to wash all this horror away.

Keeping the pistol in his right hand, he pulled out his flask with his left and gulped down several swallows. The cheap liquor burned all the way down. At this rate, he'd need to find another store to scavenge to keep up his supply.

They'd slowed down for Shay. Julio slung his arm through hers, helping her along as Shay leaned heavily on him. Still, they both lagged behind.

They made an unlikely pairing—Shay tall and willowy, at least 5'10, her wild coils framing delicate features, her rich brown skin beaded with sweat, beautiful despite the heat and her head wound;

and Julio, a heavy-set Cuban in his fifties, 5'8 at most, red-faced and huffing.

"Sorry," Julio panted. He pressed one hand over his soft, heaving belly. "I spend my days slinging bottles and concocting exotic drinks behind a bar. I'm not cut out for this."

"None of us are," Dakota said darkly.

"You're doing your best," Shay encouraged him. "You're a big help."

Dakota half-turned and shot her a pained look, but Shay was oblivious.

Dakota shook her head and lengthened her stride.

"What is that?" Dakota asked abruptly.

She strode up to a cobalt blue Ford Focus bumped over the curb at a sharp angle, both the driver and front passenger doors flung wide open. The front fender and hood were partially crushed.

The side of the car was scraped and dented in several places, like the driver had attempted to wend his way through the obstacle course of the street, banging into other cars along the way.

"What do you see?" Logan asked.

She bent over the windshield and pointed. The safety glass was cracked in a spiderweb pattern, just like a thousand other cars, but this was different. The cracks radiated out from two holes puncturing the windshield on the driver's side.

"Bullet holes," Dakota said what he was already thinking.

Logan's pulse quickened as he drew his Glock and spun around, scanning their surroundings for any potential threats. Everything looked the same. Nothing moved. The air was hot and still.

Satisfied, he returned his attention to the car but kept his weapon drawn.

"There's blood," Dakota said softly.

Logan peered into the driver's side window. The glass was

unbroken. The car keys were gone. And a dark splotch stained the tan fabric of the driver's seat.

Even in the heat, his blood went cold. "It looks like this car drove *into* the hot zone. Otherwise the glass would be shattered from the shockwave, right?"

Dakota straightened. "Right."

Logan's gaze dropped from the dark streak along the side of the seat to the droplets staining the pavement and sidewalk. They led into a side alley. The blood was dry. Logan didn't follow them.

Dakota squatted without touching anything. "And the blood stains are on top of all the dust and debris. This definitely happened after."

"Who would do something like this?" Julio asked, his tanned face going pale. "People should've been fleeing for the lives, not shooting at each other."

Dakota and Logan exchanged a hard glance. They were both thinking the same thing. "A robbery gone bad, maybe," he said. "Or a turf war."

"That Blood Outlaw thug said they were trying to take over Miami," Shay said, nibbling nervously on her thumbnail. "Could this be from that gang?"

"Could be," Logan said.

"We need to stay alert." Dakota narrowed her eyes at Logan. "All of us."

They continued on their way, all of them anxious and wary. No one wanted a repeat of Old Navy, least of all Logan.

A few minutes later, Dakota came up beside Logan, holding onto the stock of the M4 with whitened knuckles. She eyed him warily. "We still need to talk."

"Can I say no?"

Her features were taut with tension. Her long auburn waves were yanked back in a messy ponytail, and strands of damp hair clung to her forehead. "There's something you're not telling me. And that makes you a risk to the whole group."

"Nothing that's any of your business."

She glanced behind them at Julio and Shay and lowered her voice. "Were you in prison because you murdered someone?"

Irritation prickled beneath his skin. "Please see my previous response."

She flashed him a scathing look. "You aren't military, but you *are* something."

"I'm confused. Do you want me to be a killer or don't you? Because back in the store, I seem to remember a different story."

He felt her eyes on him, burning into him with their intensity. "Killing someone doesn't make you an evil person. It depends on who and why."

He said nothing, just lengthened his stride and walked faster.

Pushing down his annoyance, he glanced around, keeping his gaze constantly roaming, scanning the damaged buildings to either side and the street ahead, checking the cars and watching for movement, for danger.

He wouldn't be taken by surprise again.

"Why were you in prison?"

He sighed. She wouldn't stop unless he gave her something. "Not for murder. And not for rape. Nothing like that."

He'd gone down for assault and battery. A six-year sentence; out in three for good behavior. He'd been out of the joint for over a year now.

The murders—he'd gotten away with those, whether he wanted to or not.

He peered into the shadowed interior of a barbershop. Shattered mirrors, demolished chairs. The barber pole out front looked like a half-melted candy cane.

He felt her gaze on him, her eyes narrowed.

"Believe me or not, it's no skin off my back," he muttered.

"You didn't kill that guy when you had the chance," she said. "Is that because you have a moral compass? You look all tough, but inside you're a pathetic coward? Or were you just drunk?"

He refused to flinch, to show that she was getting to him. "You don't pull a punch, do you?"

"I can't afford to. And neither can you. Not anymore."

He shrugged. "I try to spend as much of my life as possible at the bottom of the bottle. Analyzing the complexities of life isn't exactly my forte."

"Everyone has a code. A line. I know where mine is. The question is, where's yours?"

A sharp bitterness welled on his tongue. He swallowed it down with a healthy swig of whiskey. "Things aren't so black and white."

"Sometimes they are. So, which is it? Which way does your compass point?"

"I'm still trying to figure that out." That, at least, was the truth.

They passed an elementary school with all the windows blown out but the roof intact. The playground was empty, the parking lot half-filled with teachers' cars. The owners of those cars must have abandoned everything and escaped on foot.

It was still summer break, but the sign in front of the school advertised summer school sessions. He tried not to think about the children, how the glass must have shredded into them like knives...

Clearly, he wasn't drunk enough. He took another long, burning swallow.

"Shay almost died today," Dakota said.

He stiffened. Regret bubbled up from somewhere inside him. He shoved it back down. "I'm well aware," he said sharply.

She tucked stray strands of her long hair behind her ears. "Just making sure."

"Exactly what point are you trying to make?"

She hooked her thumb toward the others stumbling several yards behind them. "Shay and Julio? They're just starting to get it. The people out there? Half of the ones still alive are sitting around waiting for the government to come and rescue them.

"I know you understand what just happened. Whatever else you are, you're also a survivor. I saw it in your eyes. I know I did.

"Whoever shot those bullet holes into that car is still out there. At least a few of the Blood Outlaw thugs don't seem to care or understand about the radiation. They're gonna be sick, out of their minds from pain and confusion, and even more dangerous than they already are.

"If they find out we killed one of theirs, we'll be the ones with targets on our backs. And it's not just the gangs. Desperate people are willing to steal and fight for what they need. So, I need to know, are we together in this?"

The words tasted like ash on his tongue. "I'm not with anyone."

She snorted. "Go it alone. Fine, I don't care. But we stand a better chance as a group, and you know it. All I'm asking is, when it all hits the fan, are you gonna have my back? Are you gonna take the shot?"

Guilt pricked him beneath his sternum. She was right, much as he hated it.

He'd always despised cowards, those without the balls to look life in the face without flinching.

What was he doing now? What had he been doing for the last four years? He was out of the joint, but he acted like he was still imprisoned, still killing time until his number was up.

Anything to keep the darkness locked up deep inside.

"Don't worry about me," he growled, and meant it. "I'll hold my own."

They walked in tense silence. Several blocks later, they saw the first bodies.

3

EDEN

E den woke with a ragged gasp.

She sat up fast, surrounded by complete darkness, her heart beating with frenzied wings against her ribcage. The nightmare still clawed at her mind, fear shuddering through her body.

She blinked furiously, but the darkness didn't fade.

Frantically, she stretched out her hands, feeling the cool ceramic sides of the tub, the soft fabric of the cushions beneath her, the rolled, nubby towel that served as her pillow.

Slowly and then all at once, it came back. Dakota's warning text. The light blast, the shaking. Then the darkness and the waiting.

She pressed her fist to her lips, holding back the broken scream that wouldn't come anyway.

She didn't know which was worse: the reality or the nightmare.

The nightmare was always the same—wading through the swamp, Dakota tugging on her arm, trying to yank her to safety as the enormous logs on the bank that weren't logs slid into the water and glided toward them.

And then the monster's jaws gaping as it lunged, seizing her with teeth gleaming razor-sharp and dragging her under, where she couldn't breathe, couldn't scream, couldn't make a single sound.

Anxiety scrabbled over her skin like spiders.

She shivered and pushed away the remnants of the nightmare, forcing herself to focus on the here and now—and her empty belly.

Her stomach cramped and knotted. Nausea roiled through her, acid stinging her throat. She'd been trapped in the darkness for over two days now. She had no food, no light, no way to communicate with the outside world, not even a voice to cry for help.

Again and again, she'd resisted the temptation to open the door and tiptoe out to the kitchen to grab a box of Corn Chex or a handful of chocolate chip granola bars from the pantry.

There was radiation outside the bathroom door. The devastating effects of the bomb. She didn't know how bad things were.

How long could she wait? How long did it take for the human body to eat itself? Would she starve to death in her own bathroom?

She had a thousand questions, and not a single answer.

Her dry, gritty mouth ached with thirst.

At least she had access to water.

She rose unsteadily from the tub, fighting off a wave of dizziness, and carefully stepped out.

In the last two days, she'd fumbled her way in the dark at least forty times, feeling the edge of the tub, the toilet seat, reaching up for the counter.

She'd scooped cool water into her mouth and prayed she wasn't accidentally poisoning herself.

Except this time.

The water she'd filled was gone. While she was sleeping, the sink had drained.

Dismayed, she sucked in her breath, fighting back a despairing sob.

She turned the "cold" handle on and held her cupped hand

beneath the faucet. Only a few dribbles splashed against the granite sink before she could catch them.

She turned the "hot" handle.

Still nothing.

She should have filled the tub with water, too. But when the initial blast had shaken the house, she'd hid inside it with the cushions over her head for protection. Utterly terrified, she hadn't dared to move for hours.

Now, fresh panic roared through her. Helpless tears burned the backs of her eyes. She opened her mouth, but no sound came out.

Eden banged angrily on the faucet, suddenly furious at it for so utterly failing her.

Her fists thudded against the cool metal. One punch missed, and her hand scraped the sharp lip of the faucet and slammed into the granite counter.

Pain stung her knuckles and sliced the side of her palm.

She clutched her hand to her heaving chest and stood in the darkness, surrounded by silence, completely alone.

Fresh sobs clawed up the back of her throat. She gasped shallow, frightened breaths, fighting back the panic threatening to swallow her whole.

No water.

She couldn't survive without it; she knew that much.

What was she supposed to do now?

4

MADDOX

The ash continued to fall from the sky. Or maybe it traveled on the wind, wafting from one raging fire to the next. It was hard to tell.

It gathered in Maddox Cage's eyelashes, accumulated on his head and shoulders. It wasn't like the fine-grained particles filming the ground, the cars, the road, covering everything everywhere he looked.

He knew that stuff was dangerous, infused with deadly radiation. He touched it as little as possible, but some things couldn't be helped.

He almost stuck out his tongue, the ash swirling temptingly like flakes of pure snow.

But this ash was anything but pure.

If he dared to taste it, the ash would sear his lips, scorch his throat.

This, too, was part of the judgment.

He'd been sitting for hours, slumped on the curb, his back resting against a parking meter as he drifted in and out of awareness.

Gradually, the piercing pain in his head lessened. The bruising ache along his ribs faded. His stomach hurt, nausea surging through his belly in waves, but he ignored it.

As he stared up at the ash, his mind finally began to clear.

He remembered who he was and where he came from. He understood everything that was happening, and why.

The holy words of the Prophet had come to pass. The Shepherds of Mercy, his father among them, were right. They had always been right.

He did not worry about the wellbeing of his father or his cousin Reuben. His father was back at the compound, far from the blast. Rueben, too, would be spared.

Reuben had known, though, hadn't he? As the Prophet's own son and one of the chosen Shepherds, he'd known about the bomb, just as he'd known Maddox was in Miami.

Reuben had sent Maddox the warning, though it hadn't come in time.

Had his father known what was coming and when?

The Prophet surely did.

Had they sent him into the danger zone to retrieve the girls anyway? Had they wanted him to fail? Was this his father's way of getting rid of him?

A flare of rage rose up in him, burning bright and painful in his chest. He stifled it swiftly.

Did it really matter?

Whatever he must suffer, he would suffer. Whatever his duty, he would do it without qualm or question.

The consequences of straying from The Way were high. Maddox had the scars to prove it.

Only suffering led to purity, to obedience. There must be death of selfishness, arrogance, and pride. There must be punishment.

The country had become polluted. Contaminated. Sickened

with a cancer that couldn't be killed without cutting it out with brutal efficiency.

To save something, sometimes you must destroy it.

Only out of the ashes could something new and pure arise.

The chosen.

The Shepherds would lead the chosen in the truth, in The Way. Only then would God bless the land, returning it to abundance and prosperity, to a new Eden on Earth.

The Shepherds were selected by God Himself, angels clothed in human form, destined to be the hands and feet of the Lord to enact judgment on His behalf.

They would bring about the new Earth. They would create the paradise that God had intended. This was the Shepherds' holy mission.

Maddox himself was not chosen to be a Shepherd. He had not deserved to be chosen.

Dakota and Eden had escaped because of him. Not once, but twice. He'd failed his father, failed the Prophet.

He knew what they would say, could see his father's rigid jaw and furious, sparking gaze in his mind's eye.

If he could not be trusted with small tasks, how could he be trusted to carry out the judgment?

Once, Maddox would've burned with fury and bitterness.

He'd always been the second-best son, the black sheep, the undisciplined one, the disappointment. His father had made that clear to him every day of his life. The prodigal son, his father had called him. *I'd rather you rotted in a pigsty than carry my name,* the man had said to him once. *Your brother will be the one who stands at my side. And you? Where will you be?*

Maddox cringed at the memory. He had hated his brother for stealing his rightful place as firstborn. Despised him for his perfect, undoubting obedience, the faith and devotion that came so easily to him, and so hard to Maddox.

But his brother was gone now. Jacob was dead. There was no bringing him back.

And Maddox had learned. He would be better. He was worthy, and he would prove it to them all. But especially, he would prove it to his father.

He wasn't angry. He wasn't jealous or vindictive.

He was resolved, resolute, unwavering.

Maddox rose to his feet and began to walk.

Now more than ever, he knew he must remain faithful. The Prophet knew the will of God. And his father, Solomon Cage, was the Prophet's own brother.

The Prophet wanted the girls. His father wanted the girls.

The task had been given to Maddox. His mission had not changed. The will of God did not change.

He could not let Dakota Sloane escape judgment. He must get Eden and bring her home.

Once he did, he would be welcomed back with open arms.

The Shepherds were merciful and forgiving.

His back bore the scars of their mercy.

Maybe he could still earn himself a place within the Shepherds of Mercy. He could still be one of them, could still bring honor to the Prophet.

Most of all, he could still make his father proud.

All was not lost.

With a fresh sense of purpose, Maddox climbed a pile of rubble and squatted before a street sign half-buried in broken concrete. North Miami Ave.

He knew this street. He could take it north almost to his destination.

The phone in his pocket was a dead hunk of metal, unusable, but he had memorized the address his father had given him.

Before the blast, he'd looked up the house on Google Earth, zeroing in as close as possible.

His target was a large, stately tan stucco home with a sparkling pool and sprawling lanai, powder-blue shutters in front, with a manicured yard fringed with elephant palms and a single bright pink flamingo stuck in the mulch—likely a concession to the girl the owners had taken in as their own.

The girl who did not belong to them.

He was less than four miles away, less than four miles from completing his mission.

He passed throngs of wretches begging for help, for redemption. He did not stop for them. He did not spare them an ounce of mercy.

These tortured souls were beyond redemption.

He knew how to find his own.

He was bruised, battered, beset with hunger, thirst, and exhaustion. His stomach churned, the headache returning.

But it didn't matter.

He was no stranger to pain.

Maddox staggered on.

5

DAKOTA

The scarf didn't block the fetid, repugnant stink from infecting Dakota's nostrils. She could taste it on the back of her tongue. Her eyes watered. She tried not to choke, her stomach nauseous.

Just outside a silver Toyota Highlander, a woman and a man covered in blood lay collapsed in the middle of the street. The hood, grill, and front bumper were a crumpled wreck of twisted metal. Flies buzzed everywhere, the noxious stench of death and decay bleeding into the air.

Shay and Julio coughed and covered their mouths.

"God help them," Julio said.

"They're beyond help," Dakota said.

"Not their souls. We can keep praying for their souls."

Dakota stared at the bodies without blinking. She wanted to turn away, to hide from the carnage, but she refused.

These people died in the same blast she'd been lucky enough to escape. The least she could do was pay her respects to the dead by bearing witness.

It mattered somehow. She believed that with every fiber of her being.

They trudged on.

As she walked, Dakota shut out the ugliness around her and concentrated on the small, cozy cabin, well-protected in the middle of the swamp, imagined her and Eden sitting at the scarred wooden table, warm and happy and safe.

How she missed that place.

It didn't matter that it wasn't large or fancy. Or that it didn't have a TV or even a microwave. Or even that they had to cut their own firewood and grow and cook their food from scratch.

She recalled old Ezra's grizzled face, his gruff smile; the way he would scowl intently whenever he was bent in concentration over his guns or ham radio, or when he instructed them in the art of survival.

She focused on the memories to push out the fear and dread prickling the back of her neck. She'd been afraid that first night, too, absolutely terrified of the crazy old survivalist that Maddox and Jacob had taught her to fear.

Ezra Burrows was not a nice man; neither was he unkind. He wasn't cruel, but he wasn't safe, either. He was plenty dangerous.

The night she and Eden had escaped the compound, they'd stolen the airboat and stumbled onto Ezra's private property.

Hungry and parched, with Eden bleeding profusely from the gash in her throat, Dakota had been desperate enough to do something stupid.

She figured the old man had a stash of supplies they could break into. Grab some food and water, maybe something for Eden's neck, then make it the rest of the way into town.

Before she'd given her the key to the exterior gates, Sister Rosemarie had pressed a wad of cash into her hands—almost a thousand dollars.

Dakota could find a cheap hotel for them, then figure out their next move. She had a vague plan to walk or hitch a ride to Everglades City. Find a payphone and call her only living relative, a grandfather on her father's side somewhere in Kentucky.

She hadn't heard from him or seen him since her parents' funeral almost seven years before. After her parents' death, her estranged aunt on her mother's side had grudgingly accepted custody, and that had been that.

Dakota barely left the compound, and certainly not to visit heathen family members. The Prophet taught that outside influences bred wickedness. And Dakota's aunt believed every word he spoke.

Aunt Ada was a severe, dour woman whose religious fervor was only surpassed by her worship of the Prophet and his grave, doom-filled prophecies.

She adored every aspect of homesteading life at the compound, equating godliness with grueling physical labor. The harder you worked, the less tempted you were to sin.

It hadn't succeeded with Dakota.

Dakota hesitated at the edge of the property, letting her eyes further adjust to the night, the darkness and the swamp at her back. There were no trees or even shrubs to hide behind.

Within four acres of the main house, the entire area had been cleared except for three smaller buildings, probably for the very reason she needed them: concealment.

Maddox had said the owner was a paranoid old fool. He'd probably shoot them on sight. Her shoulders hunched, her body tensing, half-expecting a bullet to the spine.

This was a mistake.

But her throat burned with thirst. Dizziness washed over her in waves.

Eden was making low, mangled sounds in the back of her throat, sounding more like a wounded animal than a human.

Chills darted up her spine. Something was very, very wrong.

Eden just needed a little food and water in her. Then she'd be fine. She had to be fine.

Dakota refused to accept any other alternative. If anything happened to Eden, it would be Dakota's fault.

"We're gonna make a mad dash for that shed to get some cover. If there's nothing we can use in there, then I guess we'll try the house."

That was an awful idea. She was smart enough to know it.

It was dangerous to sneak around back and try to break into the house.

More dangerous still to go directly to the front door and beg for mercy. The old man would be more likely to turn them in to the Shepherds at the compound—or shoot them—than turn them away.

No. They couldn't allow themselves to be found.

The only threat worse than getting shot was returning to the compound.

Dakota would rather die.

With that bleak thought, she grasped Eden's arm and hoisted her more firmly over her shoulder. She flinched against the spasm of pain rippling across her back.

The new burn—a dime of scorched flesh—blazed with agony as Eden's weight rubbed against it. Tears sprang into her eyes. She blinked them away.

She scanned the yard one last time, peering carefully at the overgrown grass and weeds in the shadows cast by the moon.

Would a paranoid crazy guy really plant booby traps in his own yard? She didn't know, and she didn't want to find out.

An irregularity caught her eye. Some of the blades of grass were broken, slightly tramped down. Not by much; you'd only see it if you were really looking.

She could barely make out the faintest, shadowy line between the shed and the fence near where she stood.

Paranoid or not, it was the safest option. She took off for the shed, teeth gritted against the pain searing her upper back, half-dragging Eden's considerable weight as shin-high weeds snagged her dress and scratched her legs.

An owl hooted nearby. An explosion of wings nearly gave her a heart attack as a feathered body swooped over her head with a rush of wind.

She ducked with a startled gasp.

Her heart thudded so loud in her chest she wouldn't have heard a herd of charging wild boars.

Eden groaned.

"Almost there," she whispered.

When they were still fifty yards away, a bright light switched on, bathing the yard in a harsh, white glow. Motion sensor lights.

Sweat popped out on her forehead and congealed beneath her armpits. Every hair on her arms and neck stood on end.

Should they turn back? No, it was too late now. They'd either been spotted, or they hadn't.

They needed supplies. They were desperate. She had no choice.

Feeling vulnerable and exposed, she picked up her pace, hobbling with Eden, too terrified to breathe until they reached the west flank of the shed.

Up close, it was much larger than she'd thought. Two stories of corrugated metal with four small, square windows and a set of metal doors, the handles bound with chains and a padlock.

The windows were high and too small for a body to fit through.

Carefully, she eased Eden down in the grass. Her sister slumped against the wall, barely conscious.

As the motion sensor light blared down on them, Dakota cupped her hands and peered through the small window, catching a dim glimpse of cinder block walls lined with shelves neatly stacked with containers, bins, and bags of food, water, and other supplies.

Just as Maddox and Jacob had said.

She felt around in the weeds for a rock, found one the size of her fist, and hurled it at the light fixture above her head.

It struck with a solid thwack.

The light didn't break. It was shatter-proof.

She cursed and glared up at the roof. A small red light glowered down at her from a black device anchored to the eaves beside the light.

A camera.

6

DAKOTA

Terror had zapped through Dakota. It felt like biting into a live wire.

She stiffened, anticipating the blaring alarms, the savage bark of salivating guard dogs ready to tear them limb from limb, the tell-tale click of a shotgun being cocked.

The seconds turned into a minute.

Nothing happened.

Maybe he wasn't home. Or maybe his little fortress wasn't as well defended as everyone at the compound believed.

It was a wild and desperate hope, but it was all she had.

She had to focus, to act. *One, two, three. Breathe.*

Steeling herself, she seized the rock with shaking hands and slammed it against the padlock again and again, each *crack* a cannon blast in the stillness.

She cringed but forced herself to continue.

She was committed now. Out of options.

She struck the lock again. Sparks flashed off the metal.

On the next try, her hand slipped and scraped painfully against the metal chains.

"Come on, come on, you stupid piece of—"

The padlock was open.

Dazed, she blinked back the sweat dripping into her eyes. She stared down at the padlock dumbly for several seconds, her arms already pulled back for the next blow.

Had it just snapped open? Or had it never been locked in the first place?

Hell, she was losing it.

She hadn't stopped shaking since it happened—hours ago now.

She was exhausted and scared. Every time she closed her eyes, she saw the body, the blood, the gaping mouth and empty eyes.

And then Eden, falling as if in slow motion, blood spilling from her throat like a silk ribbon.

Maybe this unlocked door was a trap. Maybe it was a gift.

Eden would say it was God looking out for them.

In that moment, Dakota didn't care.

She fumbled with the padlock and ripped off the chains. They fell into the weeds with a dull thud.

"Come on." She squatted, got her arms beneath Eden's armpits, and lifted her as much as she could, the girl's legs hanging limp as Dakota lugged her into the shed.

The burn pulsed with searing pain, but she took several deep breaths and forced herself to ignore it. Eden needed her more.

The girl's eyelids fluttered. Her skin was dead-fish white. Scarlet streaks stained her blouse from her neck to her waist.

And her throat—the shirt Dakota had tied around her neck was saturated with blood.

Dakota was afraid to remove it.

"Stay with me, okay? Stay awake." She squeezed Eden's hand and rose to her feet, turning to take in the contents of the shed.

Dozens of shelves were crowded with canned vegetables, fruits, and beans; sealed containers labeled with oats, flour, and other grains; water purification tablets and jugs of bleach; packs of batteries in all sizes; matches, hand sanitizer, and N95 air filtration masks; bottles of shampoo and body wash; even a bunch of tubes of toothpaste and plastic toothbrushes wrapped in plastic.

Everything was orderly and labeled and clean. She ran her finger along the shelf. Not even dusty.

Medical supplies lined the top shelf just above her head. Boxes of gauze, bottles of iodine, rubbing alcohol, and hydrogen peroxide, a suturing kit, sterilizing spray, topical antibiotic tubes, and a row of white medicine-sized bottles emblazoned with brightly colored fish. They were labeled "amoxicillin."

She swallowed, her throat raw with thirst. First, they needed hydration.

She snagged two cans of peaches, tugged back the lid of one, and lifted it to Eden's parched lips. "Drink. You need the energy."

Eden swallowed with a ragged moan.

"Get it down." Dakota slurped down half the can herself, syrup staining her fingers and lips. The peaches were the juiciest, sweetest things she'd ever tasted.

She pushed the can into Eden's hands and moved back to the shelves, searching for something to carry supplies in.

A few dozen reusable grocery bags were neatly folded on a lower shelf. She opened one and scooped a container of peanut butter and two more cans of peaches off the shelf. She dug into a box labeled MREs, high-calorie meal replacement pouches used in the military.

Eden made a contorted, rasping sound.

Dakota glanced at her. Eden gave a weak, barely perceptible shake of her head. Dakota knew what she meant. *No stealing.*

Dakota was no thief. But she was desperate. "Just enough to get to Copeland or Everglades City, okay? I promise."

The owner of this place had invested time, effort, and cost into procuring and storing all this stuff. Taking any of it made her feel ill.

Stealing was a grave sin at the compound, punishable by a visit to the mercy room. The welt on her back burned like it was still on fire, like drips of acid or boiling water was searing her skin.

To please Eden, she put three of the MREs back and kept only two, along with the two cans of peaches and four bottles of water. There was still plenty of room in the bag.

Eden moaned.

Dakota glanced down at her. "I know, okay? We don't have a choice."

With trembling fingers, Eden reached into the pocket of her long, filthy skirt, pulled out a folded piece of paper, and gazed beseechingly up at Dakota.

With a sigh, Dakota bent and grabbed it.

It was one of Eden's drawings—an eagle perched atop a cypress tree, its wings outspread just before it lifted into flight. Like all of her drawings, it was a nearly perfect rendition, shaded and rich with depth and beauty.

Eden wanted her to leave the drawing behind.

Dakota placed it in the empty space where she'd taken the peaches. "Like a trade, right? So it's not stealing."

The corner of Eden's lip twitched. Then her head slumped toward her chest, her eyelids flickering.

Panic clawed at Dakota's insides. She didn't know much about medical stuff, but she knew falling asleep now was a terrible idea.

She paused to shake the girl awake.

"We can't rest, not yet. We've got to get out of here." She seized a box of gauze from the shelf, a wheel of medical tape, and a tube of antibiotics. "I won't take anything else, but we can't leave that dirty shirt on you."

She stuffed the supplies into the grocery bag. "You need a fresh bandage and more water, and then we'll figure out the next step. But we shouldn't stay here. It's too dangerous—"

"That's one thing you got right," a deep, raspy growl boomed through the shed.

7

DAKOTA

Instinctively, Dakota had stepped in front of Eden, shielding her with her body. Terror coursed through her veins. She tasted her heart in her mouth.

A man stood in the doorway, silhouetted by the motion sensor light outside, a sawed-off shotgun pointed at her chest. "You little rats think you're gonna rob me?"

Ezra Burrows was a grizzled man in his late sixties, dressed in worn jeans, work boots, and a threadbare red-and-black plaid shirt. Instead of the bent old man she'd imagined, he stood tall and straight-backed, still thick and muscular, his broad shoulders straining his shirt.

"You broke into my property and stole from me," he growled in a deep, gravelly voice. Wrinkles creased his leathered face like lines in cement. "Caught you red-handed. Means I gotcha dead to rights."

He meant the Stand Your Ground law. Odds were, he could shoot them and walk away free and clear, without jail time or even a fine.

Her lungs constricted. The room blurred.

She blinked and lifted her hands slowly into the air to show she had no weapon, the bag of stolen food digging into her right shoulder.

"We did steal, sir," she stammered. "No more than we had to, but it's still wrong. Shoot me but leave her out of it. My—my sister, she's innocent. I did the stealing."

He kept the gun aimed at her chest. "I don't generally shoot little girls, not unless they got guns and are shootin' right back. I'm fixin' to call the cops to put you in a jail cell where you belong."

Her heart splintered in her chest. "I'd rather you shot me."

"What kind of answer is that? Do I look like I'm in the mood for tricks?"

"No tricks." She lifted her chin defiantly. "I'd rather be shot dead than go back to that place. Me and her both."

His eyes narrowed. A rich, vivid blue, they seemed to pierce straight through her. He took in their torn and dirty skirts and long braids, Eden's button-up blouse with the lace collar, the once-pristine fabric now soaked a bloody red-black.

His stony face betrayed no emotion. "You're from that River Grass Compound. You're those Shepherds of Mercy freaks."

"Was." She spat out the word like it was poisoned.

He gestured at the bag with his shotgun. "Spill it."

"We'll give it back—everything but the one can of peaches and bottle of water we already used. We'll get out of your hair and be gone, and you won't ever see or hear from us again, I promise you that."

"Shut your yammering and let me see exactly what you stole from me."

Dakota dumped the bag. The cans and waters rolled across the wooden plank floor. A bottle of water came to rest against the man's steel-toed boot.

"We took just enough to get by. No more. We're not thieves."

"I'll be the judge of that." His hard gaze flicked over her head. "What's that on the shelf?"

"My—sister, she wanted to give you something, a trade so it didn't feel like stealing. I know it still was—"

"Show me."

She reached behind her for the shelf, her quivering hands betraying her fear, and held up the drawing of the eagle.

For a long moment, he didn't say anything, just stared at it.

She stood there, not daring to move, willing the paper not to shake in her hands. She was sixteen, damn it, but she felt like she was six again and terrified of the boogie man beneath the bed.

Ezra Burrows scratched his heavily whiskered jaw. "The little girl did that?"

"Yes, sir."

Eden opened her eyes and let out a ragged gasp. She coughed, nearly choking, and made a terrible anguished, gurgling sound.

Dakota nearly stopped breathing. It was like all the air had been sucked out of the room. How badly wounded was she? What had Dakota done?

"What's all the blood from?" the man asked.

She opened her mouth, but nothing came out.

A vision of the body flashed before her eyes—the blood spraying everywhere, the wide staring eyes, the knife clattering to the floor, covered in dripping red.

Shame and remorse wormed inside her gut. She would give nearly anything to go back and relive the last several hours over again. She saw every glaring mistake, every misstep, with blood-red clarity.

All the ways she could have done better. The truth she should've seen a long time ago. She'd been too stupid, too naïve to see the facts staring her straight in the face.

Trusting the wrong person had cost her nearly everything.

It had nearly killed Eden. Would kill her, if Dakota didn't do something soon.

What was done was done. She couldn't go back and fix it. There was only now. There was only moving forward.

"What happened?" he asked.

The old man stared at her like he could see every lie and secret tangled in her heart laid out plain as day. She sensed that if she lied, he would know it somehow.

And that would seal their fate.

Better to be vague and hope he didn't demand the truth.

"She's hurt," Dakota forced out. "Pretty bad."

He hesitated, as if weighing whether to require a more thorough answer. His jaw worked like he was chewing tobacco. A shadow passed across his craggy features.

Dakota's heart felt like it would pound right out of her chest.

After a moment, he dropped his eyes and glowered down at his shotgun. "Suppose I should call an ambulance."

"No!"

That intent, penetrating gaze focused on her again.

"Please." Her chest wound tighter and tighter, her lungs compressed in bands of iron. Her breath came in sharp, shallow gasps. "No hospitals."

A hospital was exactly what Eden needed.

But Solomon Cage and his Shepherds had a far reach. One was a local county sheriff. Another a doctor at the nearest hospital.

As soon as Eden was entered into the system, they'd know.

And they'd come for her.

Dakota hadn't risked both their lives just to go back. Sister Rose-marie hadn't risked so much to get them out for it to end like this.

She hadn't exaggerated. Death was better than that place for Eden. And for her. She'd rather die right here.

At least they'd be free.

"Please." She hated herself for begging, but desperation spurred her on. "We need your help."

His shrewd gaze skipped from the drawing to the bottle at his feet to Eden.

Eden tried to sit up. Her movements were slow and clumsy, her pallor gray. Fresh blood leaked through the cloth wrapped around her neck. Her lids fluttered, and her eyes rolled wildly into the back of her head.

Dakota could barely make out the rise and fall of her chest. She looked half-dead.

There wasn't a thing Dakota could do to stop it, nothing except put her life—and Eden's—in the hands of a hostile, possibly dangerous, stranger.

She held her blood-streaked hands palms up, beseeching, pleading with every fiber of her being. "She's gonna die if you don't help her."

"That's none of my—"

"I'll work to earn our keep. I know how to clean, mend clothes, and cook well enough to get by. I'm not afraid of hard labor. Whatever you say, I'll do it—"

"Can she walk?"

She glanced down at Eden. She was unconscious now, sagging against the shelves. Her head lolled. "I—I don't think so."

The old man worked his jaw again for a moment, as if he were engaged in an internal debate with himself. The shadow cleared from his features.

With a heavy sigh, he leaned his shotgun against the wall. "Come on, then. Keep yourself in plain sight, right in front of me at all times. Any funny business and I'll be shooting now, askin' questions later."

Dakota tensed, frozen, unsure whether to believe what she'd just heard.

Ezra had lifted Eden in his arms as easily as a kitten and strode out of the barn. "Take your filthy boots off before you get in the house. I just waxed the floors."

Hope jolted to life within her chest. "Yeah, okay. I can do that! Thank—"

Ezra hadn't broken his stride as he'd growled over his shoulder, "And bring the suture kit on the shelf behind you."

She still remembered the palpable relief that had flooded through every cell in her body as she'd hurried after the old man, too consumed with concern for Eden to worry about her own safety.

Dakota smiled grimly at the memory. She'd been terrified of Ezra that first night.

Now she couldn't wait to get back to him.

She missed him and that cabin with a physical ache beneath her ribs.

Her foot struck a chunk of drywall the size of a large screen TV, thrusting her sharply back to the present.

She nearly tripped, her heart juddering, arm flailing, and caught herself with the side window of a platinum gray Volkswagen Jetta parked sideways in the middle of the road.

"You okay?" Shay asked from behind her.

"Fine," she lied. Heart still banging against her ribs, she glanced up as the group veered around several abandoned cars.

Off to the right, a billboard was broken off halfway up the side of a large, three-story office building. The advertisement was for a dentist's office, the image of a young blonde girl with a blinding white smile split right down the center.

Something about the girl reminded her of Eden.

Dakota kept staring at the broken sign, at the tragic, splintered smile, kept seeing it in her mind—even after they'd left it far behind.

They crossed a side road and turned onto West Biscayne Street, a wide thoroughfare lined with art boutiques, specialty shops and cafes, and hip, low-rise condos.

Or at least, it used to be.

Dakota jerked to a stop, stunned.

8

LOGAN

Logan stared in shock.

Shay gasped and covered her mouth with her fingers.

"Mother Mary and Joseph," Julio murmured.

As the initial blast had radiated outward from ground zero, the shockwaves rebounding off varying surfaces—tall buildings, the terrain, maybe even the atmosphere—had struck this section of the city much harder than the Beer Shack on Front Street.

Without the protection of the larger, taller buildings, the smaller shops, restaurants, and apartments here had suffered significant damage.

Half of them were destroyed. The remaining buildings were hunched and broken. In the distance, at least a dozen structures were only burned and blackened husks, smoke pouring into the sky.

Rubble heaped here and there: concrete in jagged mounds, ruptured asphalt, scattered fragments of plastic, paper, and detritus; fallen electric lines.

And the bodies—bodies were everywhere.

The foul, reeking stench of decomposing flesh in the blistering heat was nearly overwhelming. And beneath that was the scorched odor of burnt plastic, rubber, and other things Logan didn't want to think about.

Behind him, Julio retched.

"Go," Dakota whispered, her voice raw. "I know it's awful, but we've got to move."

Jolted out of his shock, Logan made his way carefully down the street. He scanned to the left and right for signs of potential trouble. The more he saw, the more he longed to turn and flee.

Gingerly, they moved around the skeletons of cars and mounds of still-smoking rubble, picking their way through the debris—more glass, chunks of twisted metal, crumbled brick and masonry.

A few groans and agonized cries echoed weakly ahead of them.

People were still trapped inside the buildings. They were wounded, in terrible agony, likely dying.

Dozens, maybe hundreds of people.

The terrible realization struck him like a swift kick to the balls. He felt like the air had been knocked right out of him.

Logan jerked out his flask, unscrewed the lid, and knocked back a long swallow.

Dakota shot him a scathing look. "Now? Really?"

He didn't bother to answer her, just downed another drink and wiped his mouth with the back of his arm. As far as he was concerned, the faster the booze blunted his senses, the better.

He'd choose a coma over this hell.

"Where are the first responders?" Julio's eyes widened in dismay. "Where are the firefighters and EMTs and the National Guard? Where is the help?"

Dakota pointed at the stalled and crashed vehicles surrounding them. "How can an ambulance or fire truck even get through? Every road is impassable. Closer to ground zero, you can add mountains of rubble and collapsed buildings to the mix. Responders will have to hike in by foot or drop by chopper."

"I'm sure they're out here," Logan said. "But they'll need personal protection equipment. Otherwise, they're sacrificing themselves."

"The suits only shield them from alpha and beta rays that can't penetrate clothing," Dakota said, "not gamma radiation. Any responders who brave the hot zone are risking their own health."

"It'll take weeks—months, maybe—to sift through all this." Shay's voice trembled.

Gone was the perkiness, the trite positivity. Whether it was the gunshot or the horrors surrounding them, reality seemed to have finally hit her—and hard. "So many people will die waiting for help..."

Help that wouldn't come in time.

The numbers were mind-numbing. And there were more bombs, more devastated cities. How would Miami ever recover from such a catastrophic blow? Washington D.C.? New York City?

The entire country?

It was almost too much to take in. Logan's brain kept trying to reject the information, to deny the horror right in front of him.

But there was no way to deny this.

He guzzled another slug of whiskey. Warmth seeped into his belly. But it wasn't enough. An IV of vodka mainlined straight into his veins wouldn't be enough.

"There must be something we can do," Shay said, aghast.

"What?" Logan said dully. "How?"

Shay gnawed on her thumbnail, her eyes shiny with tears. "Go in and free the people who are trapped. Dig them out of the rubble..."

Dakota gestured at a Starbucks across the street. The western wall had caved in. Mounds of rubble at least three feet high spilled out the front door. "With what tools? We don't have protective suits. Every time we touch something, we're contaminating ourselves."

"Every hour we stay out here, we just expose ourselves to further radiation," Logan said. "We have to get ourselves out alive. That's all we can do."

A groan from the right drew his attention.

Only ten feet to their right, an Asian bistro's roof had fallen in, great chunks of it cascading over the outdoor seating area, the wooden chairs and tables splintered like kindling.

Several bodies were trapped beneath the rubble. All dead.

A flash of movement caught his eye.

"Someone's alive over here!" He strode closer, his stomach churning violently. He dreaded what he would see. He forced himself to look anyway.

A Cuban woman in her thirties lay on the brick paver patio. The roof had collapsed on top of her; her legs from the thighs down were crushed.

Splintered bone poked from the mangled flesh, blood staining her khaki shorts and rose-pink shirt. A five-foot spear of rebar pierced her chest just above her heart, pinning her to the bricks.

The woman managed to lift her head. Her black, curly hair spread around her like a halo. She clutched a bundle of something against the uninjured side of her chest.

Her pain-bleary gaze met Logan's.

"*Por favor,*" she whispered.

Behind him, Shay and Julio hobbled closer.

Shay gasped. "She's alive!"

He took a step closer. Only now could he make out the object she cradled in her arms. A tiny face peeked out of the bundled cloth.

For a split second, he let himself hope the baby still lived. Then he saw the shard of glass longer than his forearm jutting from the infant's fragile neck.

The baby—a boy, by the pale blue blanket wrapped around his tiny form—was dead.

9

LOGAN

Revulsion roiled through Logan. He stumbled back in horror.
The baby's blank, lifeless eyes bored straight to the center of his soul.

In the blast, the glass from all the windows and doors had transformed into weapons. Thousands of glass shards hurled like javelins, lancing into vulnerable, defenseless flesh.

"Please," the woman begged in a ragged whisper, her voice a ghost of itself. Her eyes were hollowed out, her face a husk, a mask of something human whose humanity had been wrung from it by suffering and grief.

It hurt to look at her.

A helpless, impotent rage filled him.

His free hand balled into a fist at his side. He wanted to hurt whoever had done this, whatever monstrous rogue state or terrorist entity had so callously destroyed something so innocent as a child.

Like you did? the voice in his head whispered.

He shoved that thought down with brutal fury.

It wasn't the same. He wasn't the same.

But that was a lie.

He guzzled a long, frantic drink, desperate for the burn as it slid down his throat, the warm buzz in his veins, the forgetting.

"*Por favor*," the woman rasped again.

He knew what she was asking, what she needed.

There was no hope for her. She'd been trapped here for two days, forced to die slowly, in agony while she cradled her dead child in her arms.

He couldn't even begin to imagine the torment.

Only one thing could help her now.

Logan switched the flask to his left hand and reached beneath his shirt to unholster his Glock.

He didn't aim it at the woman. He couldn't.

Dakota turned to Logan, no doubt in her expression, no hesitation in her voice. Her eyes shone with bleak determination. "Do it."

"It's murder!" Appalled, Julio crossed himself again and shook his head. "You can't."

Leaning against Julio to steady herself, Shay hugged her arms around her ribcage, shivering despite the oppressive heat. "You're not actually thinking about it, are you?"

Dakota gestured at the woman's shattered legs beneath the ledge of heavy roof, the spear of rebar piercing her chest. "You know as well as I do that she's not gonna make it. She's in unbearable agony. She could stay alive for hours, for days, suffering."

"No," Shay said. "We can't."

"Helping her end it is merciful, a release."

"I'm a nurse!" Shay cried. "The first rule is 'Do No Harm'!"

Dakota whirled on her. "Don't you get it? That's what we're doing. We don't have morphine drips and hospice care here!"

"But she's a—"

Dakota fisted her hands on her hips. "She's a what? A woman? A mother of a dead baby? Would you say the same if it were a man?"

Shay's mouth contorted. "Yes! I know things look bad now, but rescue teams could arrive at any minute!"

"Do you see any rescuers?"

"That doesn't mean they aren't coming!"

Dakota lowered her voice. "There's no hope for her, and you know it."

"As long as she's alive, there's still hope!"

"As a person of medicine, you should know better than that."

"It's still wrong!"

"No." Dakota's whole face blazed with conviction, with a dauntless certainty Logan admired, even envied. "It's a mercy."

"But—"

"It's her decision! Not yours!" Dakota snapped. "You don't get to make that choice for her. You don't. I won't let you."

Finally, Shay shook her head in frustrated resignation and said nothing.

Logan heard them as if from far away. He couldn't tear his gaze from the dead baby, from the mother's desolate eyes.

A suffocating shame strangled his throat, as if he had done this terrible thing himself.

He gulped down another slug of whiskey.

"It's still suicide if you ask for it," Julio said, his face grave. "Don't you want to be in heaven with your child?"

Julio half-turned as he spoke to the woman, not fully looking at her. Maybe he was afraid the sight of the blood would make him faint.

Or maybe he feared staring death in the face.

Logan had seen death too many times, mostly by his own hand.

He'd thought he no longer feared it. He was wrong.

The woman didn't respond. She only groaned, in too much pain to force out more words. She clutched the child tightly to her chest.

"You can't put your religion on someone else," Dakota said

fiercely. "She asked for this. We can't help everyone. We can't do a damn thing about anything, but we can do this. This one thing."

"I'd want someone to do the same for me," Logan said quietly.

"Then do it," Dakota said.

Still, he hesitated.

He wasn't any good at keeping promises. How many times had he promised himself he'd stop drinking, only to shadow the doorway of a bar the very next day, or wake up hung-over and miserable a week later?

This was the only promise he'd managed to keep for four years, one month, and seventeen days. Even in prison, he'd beaten men unconscious, but never killed anyone.

He hadn't outright killed Blood Outlaw or his accomplice, though he should have.

The echoes of the mother's screams from that terrible night seared through his mind. The fear on her face—her fear of *him*—and the child she hid behind her, protecting him with her body, with her life.

It hadn't done either of them any good.

His gut twisted, filling him with that familiar wretchedness, that nauseous cocktail of guilt, self-loathing, and regret that only relented at the bottom of a bottle.

This was different. He knew that.

His finger twitched on the trigger guard.

And yet—

Pulling the trigger still felt like a betrayal. Even this, a mercy killing, was crossing some invisible boundary that had kept him—and the darkness inside him—safely hemmed all these years.

A heavy, helpless emptiness settled deep in his bones.

Part of him knew he needed to do it. The other part wasn't ready.

He couldn't pull the trigger.

Instead, he knocked back another drink.

Dakota swore under her breath. When she spoke, her voice was edged with steel. "Give it to me."

Relenting, he handed her the gun.

She crouched beside the woman and carefully touched the muzzle of the pistol against the side of her bloodied head.

Dakota's gaze gentled. "Are you sure?"

The woman managed a slight nod of her chin, her eyes squeezed shut as she stroked her baby's tiny skull, his blood-matted fringe of black hair.

Shay and Julio turned away when Dakota pulled the trigger.

Logan didn't.

The crack echoed in the still, humid air.

For a long moment, nothing moved. No one spoke. The silence closed in on them, stifling and oppressive.

Dakota stood heavily, her face pale, her dark eyes glistening. Sweat dripped down her temples. She didn't wipe it away.

She'd acted so sure of herself, but she was clearly shaken.

He wanted to tell her death left a stain on your soul—no matter who it was, no matter how noble the reasons.

He wanted to tell her that you never forgot the faces, the wide, terrified eyes, the way the light drained out of them like a snuffed candle.

It stayed with you forever, haunting your dreams, stalking your waking moments, just waiting to ambush you.

You learned to live with it, like a scar or a limp.

Or you tried to drown it with booze.

He wanted to tell her that he understood.

The words disintegrated to dust in his mouth. He said nothing.

The buzz hit him then, sweet relief sliding through his veins. The tension gripping him relaxed. The world softened, the sharp edge of horror blurring.

For some reason, he only felt worse.

Dakota faced away from them for a long moment, her shoulders quaking. Even Shay knew to leave her in peace. She inhaled several steadying breaths before turning around.

Her eyes were dry, her expression composed.

Fresh shame pricked him. She was stronger than he'd given her credit for. Stronger than he was.

The pistol still gripped in her hands, Dakota hesitated.

He knew she wanted to keep it; he could read it all over her face. He held out his hand and waited to see what she would do.

Slowly, as if it pained her, she handed him the pistol.

For a moment, their gazes met. He didn't like what he saw there —his own pathetic reflection in her dark, reproachful eyes.

She had judged him and found him wanting.

And rightly so.

10

DAKOTA

The heat beat down on Dakota's head, oppressive and unrelenting. The sun arced slowly across the sky, a white-hot circle burning a bright hole through the smoky haze.

South Florida was suffering a drought; not even the regular afternoon thunderstorms had offered relief in nearly two weeks. Today wouldn't break that pattern.

Dakota licked her chapped lips, swallowing to wet her dry throat.

She tried to conserve her water, but it was just too hot. She went through one bottle of water and started on a second.

Weaving between cars, rubble-strewn sidewalks, and damaged buildings was harder—and took much longer—than Dakota had anticipated.

They came across a collapsed five-story apartment that completely blocked the road. The shattered building was far too unstable to try to cross. The fires burning in the rubble had spread to nearby shops.

After backtracking two blocks and heading north again, even more fires blocked their path. Just the sight of the flames constricted her chest. Her breath hitched, all the old memories tightening like fingers around her throat, threatening to strangle her.

An hour passed. Then another.

By the time they were back on track, it was already after 4:15 p.m. They still needed to get her sister and flee the hot zone within the next few hours.

They trudged on in silence, too miserable to talk.

Smoke billowed into the sky above them. The occasional cry or moan drifted from the buildings on either side of the street. Their despair and anguish echoed inside her skull, sank into her bones.

Dakota longed to clamp her hands over her ears to block them out. It was like walking through Dante's circles of Hell, like traveling through Hades itself.

The only thing that kept her going was Eden.

Eden was the reason she even knew about *Dante's Inferno* and all the ancient Greek myths. At the compound, the women weren't allowed to read anything but certain texts from the Bible and the writings of the Prophet.

But Eden's foster parents gave her books whenever she asked for them. When Eden was finished, she passed them on to Dakota during their visits.

Dakota wanted to resent them for it—it was just another way they were buying Eden's affection—but the books were damn good. Despite her best intentions, she enjoyed them.

"Gotta take a piss break," Logan muttered.

He veered off and ducked inside a convenience store with both doors busted open.

Dakota shook her head in disgust. Searching for booze was more like it.

This time, she was hard-pressed to fault him for it. She'd drink a gallon of Windex to eradicate the wretched cries drilling into her brain.

Shay swayed a bit on her feet. "We should wait for him."

Julio tightened his grip around her waist to steady her, his brow wrinkled in concern. "You okay?"

"Yeah. I'm fine. It's just the humidity, I think."

Julio pointed at a toppled wrought-iron table on the sidewalk that had crashed through the windows of the pizza joint on their left. "Shay needs a break for a few minutes. Is this safe?"

"Our clothes will protect us from the radioactive dust," Dakota said. "But we should still wipe it down with the alcohol wipes. And don't touch anything with your bare skin."

She took out a pack of wipes and cleaned off the table and four chairs. Julio and Shay helped, Shay leaning her hip against the table for balance.

Julio pulled his sleeves over his hands and righted the table. Dakota did the same and dragged the cleaned chairs over.

They sat, resting their sore, exhausted legs, hardly moving in the blistering heat.

"How's your head?" Julio asked Shay as he pulled a couple bags of half-melted M&Ms out of his sequined bag. He opened one carefully with his sleeves still pulled over his hands, tilted his head back, and spilled them into his mouth without touching the candies themselves.

Dakota slumped in the hard metal chair. She adjusted the strap of the M4 and settled it in her lap. She passed on the candy. She had no appetite. It was too hot.

Shay patted her halo of tight, springy coils until she reached the shaved section on the right half of her scalp. She touched the bandage gingerly. It was still white, only the faintest blush of red seeping through. "I'm good for now. It hurts, but it's manageable."

Sweat beaded her brown skin and trickled down her temple, though they were all sweating. Her pallor was a bit sickly, and her eyes were red. She kept blinking.

She raised her hands toward her face like she was going to rub her eyes.

"Don't touch your face!" Dakota said sharply.

Shay flinched. "Oh, sorry."

"Don't touch your face, but especially your eyes, mouth, or nose," Dakota warned. "Accidental contamination."

"Right." Shay grimaced. She propped her clothed elbows on the table and held her hands in the air, away from her face. "It's such a habit. I didn't realize how often I touch my face for no reason. I don't even think about it."

"Your eyes are bloodshot," Julio said. "Is that a symptom of something?"

"It's my contacts. I've been wearing them for over almost three days now. Never thought I'd miss my glasses so much."

"Can you take them out?" Julio asked.

"Yeah, but I'm practically blind without them. It's fine." She laughed shakily. "Nothing like getting shot in the head, right?"

"You're doing fine," Julio said.

"I'm just ready to get back to civilization. I'm sure I'll feel better with a warm bed and a hot shower, you know?"

Dakota ran her tongue over her fuzzy teeth. It was a toothbrush she wanted most. She should have grabbed one at the Walgreens, but it had completely slipped her mind. She'd had one in her bug out bag. Packing it seemed like a lifetime ago, now.

"Just when do you think that's going to happen?" she asked.

"Soon, I hope," Shay said.

Dakota didn't bother to respond. She scanned the nearby buildings and streets—for danger, a Blood Outlaw or Maddox or another threat to materialize out of thin air—or maybe for another suffering victim to crawl out of the wreckage begging for help.

Maybe it was some of both.

Her hands curled into fists on her lap. They were still trembling after what she'd done to help that woman.

She couldn't find words for the awfulness of it: to pull the trigger and feel the thrumming jolt all the way up her arms, to watch the light fade from the woman's devastated eyes, the anguished expression etched on her face.

"It's only been a couple of days," Shay said with forced cheerfulness. "There's still time. The government will send in the National Guard to come in and rescue all these people. I'm sure of it. They're just waiting for the radiation to go down, like us."

Where she'd managed to dredge up this terrible optimism, Dakota had no idea. She just stared at her, incredulous. "You've got to be joking."

"We can't lose hope." Shay carefully took the M&Ms from Julio and smoothed the wrinkled brown bag between her fingers. She didn't eat any, just stared down at it with red-rimmed eyes and a small half-smile. "My mom says things always look better in the morning."

"How do they look for that dead mother and her baby?"

Shay pressed her lips together. "I'm just trying to think positive, okay?"

Anger flashed through Dakota, hard and fast. "You're acting like everything's fine when the world's crashing down all around you!"

Julio shot her a warning look. She ignored him.

She waved her arms, encompassing the ruins surrounding them. "You know better than I do that all these trapped people can't survive another day without water, even if their injuries and the radiation aren't enough to kill them. I know you know that."

Shay went still, that half-smile frozen on her face. "I do know."

"Really? Because you're not acting like it."

"Dakota—" Julio started.

"It's fine," Shay said.

"It's not fine!" Dakota exploded.

Anger flushed through her—a part of her knew it was irrational, but she couldn't help herself. She kept seeing that dead baby, that mother's desperate, tortured gaze locked onto her own.

"It's not okay! You have to see things the way they are, not the way you want them to be! Anything else is stupidity. And stupid gets people killed."

"That's enough!" Julio spread out his hands between them, like he was blocking a physical fight. He shot Dakota a pleading look. "Attacking each other isn't going to do anyone any good."

"No, it's okay." Shay dipped her chin graciously. "I understand where she's coming from."

Dakota snorted. "Like you understand anything!"

There was a tightness in her chest, a pressure building behind her sternum that she was helpless to stop. "You're a rich princess with your future all laid out for you, nice and perfect—a fancy college and a nice house with a fenced yard and a two-car garage—"

"Enough!" Shay stood abruptly, the chair clattering to the pavement behind her.

11

DAKOTA

Dakota stared up at Shay, momentarily speechless.

Shay swayed a bit. "Now wait just a minute. You don't know me. You don't know anything about me."

"Shay—" Julio reached out to steady her, but she waved him away.

The smile dropped from her face. Her normally placid expression contorted in anger. "Yeah, I've got some good things in my life. You know what I don't have? A dad. Because when I was sixteen, he went into our fancy two-car garage, put his gun in his mouth, and shot himself."

Dakota rocked back in her chair, stunned. Guilt skewered her. She sucked in a sharp breath. "I—I didn't know."

Shay's mouth trembled. She lifted one hand and pressed her fingers against her lips, but she kept her composure. "How could you have? But maybe give people the benefit of the doubt once in a while. Yeah, there's a lot of assholes in the world. I get it. I wasn't born yesterday.

"But I choose joy, okay? I could've let my dad's suicide destroy me, like he let his bipolar disorder destroy him. I had a choice, just like we all have a choice on how we're going to live our lives. I choose to be happy. I choose to see the joy in life, in spite of the crap. If I want to focus on the good, on hope—no matter how minuscule it is—then that's what I'm going to do."

She hesitated, as if debating whether to speak more. Her chin lifted. "And you—you don't get to sit there and judge me."

Dakota had no response.

Part of her wanted to snap right back with some snarky, smart-ass retort. Slap up the barriers and to hell with everyone else. Unleash all her pent-up fear, anger, and despair at this girl who just happened to be a convenient punching bag.

Another, more reasonable voice in her head argued for restraint.

She'd misjudged Shay more than once now. That was on her.

Shay wasn't the enemy, anyway. She wasn't the bad guy here, even when she was irritating as hell.

Everyone's nerves were on edge. They were all stressed, tense, barely keeping it together. This journey had already become more harrowing than Dakota could've imagined.

Julio was right. Arguing over nothing only drained their precious energy and distracted them from the real threats.

Julio scooted over and righted Shay's chair. She sank back into her seat with a grateful smile.

The three of them sat there in a long, uncomfortable silence.

The only sounds were the occasional distant moans of the suffering and the buzzing of flies in the humid air.

Julio reached across the table and covered Shay's hand with his. "I'm sorry for your loss. Truly."

"I've come to terms with it," Shay said quietly. "But thank you."

Dakota crossed her arms over her chest and glared down at the table. Eden always told her she was too stubborn. Admitting she was wrong was like pulling teeth.

Jeez, she missed that girl.

Eden was her compass, her north star. She felt lost without her, like she was unraveling, piece by piece.

"I shouldn't have jumped down your throat," she muttered finally.

Shay beamed at her. "Apology accepted."

They were quiet for a minute.

Shay took a long drink from her water. Her expression grew serious. "My mother is pathologically cheerful. She ignored all my dad's symptoms, like if she pretended hard enough that everything was okay, it would be. I tried to talk to her. But she refused to listen.

"She made excuses for him, said his back pain from working construction kept him in bed for weeks at a time, even after he lost his foreman job for missing so much work...She kept saying he was fine, that I was just trying to create drama and inflate my own ego by throwing around medical terms..."

She shook her head. "Those last few weeks, he suddenly started acting giddy. He gave his prize toolset away to a friend. He started saying he was going to take us to Disney World, even though he had social anxiety and loathed crowds. She just pretended it was all normal. She just wanted to live in a fantasy world. Until it was too late.

"Maybe...maybe if she'd acknowledged the warning signs, he'd still be here. I—I don't want to be like that, either."

Julio squeezed her hand in encouragement. "Don't worry. You aren't."

"Everything is—I'm just having a hard time wrapping my head around things, you know? The bombs, all this destruction, the suffering people, and no one here to help them. It's not how it's supposed to be."

"No," Dakota said quietly, "It's not."

No one said anything after that. What was there to say?

Dakota shifted uncomfortably and glanced down at her watch.

They'd been here for far too long. It was time to get moving. "Where the heck is—"

"Right here." Logan strode out of the convenience store carrying a six-pack in one hand and a small package in the other. "No water left, but plenty of happy juice."

Dakota raised her brows. "Happy juice?"

He gave a careless shrug. "Something in this damn hellhole needs to bring a bit of happiness. Otherwise, what's the point? You wanna join in the fun?"

"I'm surprised you're offering to share," Dakota said.

"Don't you know? I'm full of surprises." Logan tossed a pack of gum on the table for Shay. "Thought you might like this."

"Thank you!" Shay snatched it up. "You're a lifesaver."

He glanced around the table at the somber faces. "What'd I miss?"

Shay winked at Dakota as she tore into the gum. "Nothing too crucial."

Logan came around to Dakota's side. She smelled the alcohol on his breath. His rough cheeks were flushed, his eyes shiny.

Instinctively, she shied away as he leaned over her, her hand already going for her knife.

But all he did was pull a thick, folded paper out of his pocket and slap it on the table in front of her. He straightened. "Look at this. I found us an actual map."

Dakota's heart banged against her ribs. She released the hilt of the knife with a sharp exhale. There was no threat.

Rather, Logan had brought them something good for a change. She'd been worried about how they'd navigate without GPS once they'd rescued Eden.

She unfolded the map, spread it out on the table, and pointed to a spot just below and to the west of Wynwood. "We're here." She tapped a spot a quarter inch northwest. "Here's Eden. After we get her, we head west a couple of miles to escape the radiation and find a working hotel for the night if we can."

"How do we know when we're out of the hot zone?" Logan asked.

"Without a Geiger counter, we don't for sure," Dakota said. "I think a couple miles west will get us clear. We'll go as far as we can and then find shelter before dark. Hopefully, we'll run into some first responders, police, EMTs, or firefighters by that point."

"And after that?" Shay asked with a snap of her gum.

"Tomorrow, we should be clear enough of the rubble to find a car or bikes to travel faster," Dakota said.

She'd love to get her hands on a radio for news. A ham radio, if she were really lucky. She knew Ezra's call sign. If she could contact him, things would be so much easier.

And any ham operator worth their salt would be able to tell them what the hell was going on.

"We need to head here to get to the Trail." Dakota's finger edged through dense suburbia—through Little Havana, past the airport, the International and Dolphin malls, and IKEA to the Dade Corners Travel Center at the edge of the Glades. "Just about twenty miles."

The Travel Center was a one-stop shop for gas, propane, fishing rods, camo gear, and of course, preserved gator heads and mugs in the shape of boobs.

She planned to stock up on supplies there—if there was anything left. Hopefully, the masses had stuck to Costco and Sam's Club and left it alone.

Nearby, the Trail Glades Range offered a tempting array of weapons. If everything went as planned, she could return to Ezra with his favorite gift as a peace offering—a new rifle. At least she had the M4 to offer him.

If the road was blocked with cars, she could always steal an airboat from Coopertown, a few miles west. She knew how to operate one, and how to get close enough to Ezra's to hike in.

No one else needed to know that.

Except for Julio, two days ago, they'd all been strangers. Still, she felt responsible for Julio and Shay. They were risking themselves to help her get to Eden.

And they trusted her to get them out of the hot zone safely.

The world was going to hell, but she wasn't going down with it.

And she wasn't planning on letting it happen to anyone on her watch, either.

She'd help Shay until they found her a hospital, leaving her in good hands. Once they hit the airport, Julio would break off on his own to find his wife anyway.

As for Logan, if he got the stick out of his ass, he'd help her protect Eden until they reached the Travel Center. Then she and Eden would sneak off and leave him to his own devices.

She didn't worry about him the way she did with the others. Logan would survive just fine. She pushed down the guilt. Unlike Shay and Julio, she didn't owe Logan Garcia a damn thing.

"What's that sound?" Shay whispered.

Dakota looked up from the map. It took a moment for her brain to translate what her ears were hearing, so incongruous was it to their surroundings.

As they listened, the sound grew louder. And closer.

A car engine. And with it, music.

Dakota's heart turned to ice inside her chest. She rose from her seat, already reaching for her knife. "Hide!"

12

LOGAN

L ogan stood stock still, straining to listen. The music was a loud, thumping bass over the growl of an engine. It was coming from the northwest. And it was definitely coming closer.

"What do we do?" Julio asked as he helped Shay to her feet.

He glanced up the boulevard. While there were still crashed and abandoned cars, the road was wide enough for a car or two to weave through. No one would be going sixty miles an hour, but they could make it.

"I can think of a group who would hang around and play music," Dakota said darkly.

"It's either the Blood Outlaws or someone just as crazy or stupid," Logan said. "Either way, we don't want a meet and greet. We need to get out of here."

He had no idea how many were in the oncoming car, or even if there were more than one vehicle. Waiting to see if they were hostile was idiotic. Taking on an unknown number of hostiles from an unprotected, indefensible position was even worse.

He twisted, scanning up and down the street. The storefronts to his right were connected for thirty yards in either direction, with no side alleys to escape through. They were small, one-room businesses that offered little cover or protection.

Across the street stood a First Federal Credit Union of Florida, a hair salon, a dry cleaners, and a four-story suite of offices. "The office! Hurry!"

Logan and Dakota sprinted across the street, dodging a white Kia Rio and a dented forest green Mazda3. The doors were glass—and broken, along with the windows, but the main façade was brick, thick enough to hide them and provide cover from hostile fire if it came to that. The large sign affixed to the front of the building read "Palm Industrial Center."

The engine grew louder. It was coming from the side street ahead on the right, just north of the credit union on the corner.

Dakota slipped inside and pressed herself against the side wall out of sight. Logan followed and shrank back against the opposite wall, Glock in the low ready position.

They could hear someone laughing now, loud and maniacal over the thumping music. The car was close, about to turn.

Head north, head north, he chanted in his head, already knowing with a sinking certainty that the car would turn south toward them. Of course it would.

"Where are they?" Dakota whispered.

Logan cursed under his breath. Keeping his back against the wall, he turned and glanced out the doorway.

Julio had Shay around the waist, her arm draped across her shoulder, as they hobbled toward the safety of the building. They were still halfway across the street.

Julio froze. Shay's eyes widened in terror.

"Get down!" Logan hissed frantically. "Beneath the car!"

The nearest vehicle was a bright yellow Jeep Renegade on the office side of the street, only a few feet from the curb and even less from Shay and Julio.

Shay came to life first. She grabbed Julio's arm and dove for the pavement. Shay rolled beneath the undercarriage, ducking her head to miss the front wheel.

Julio dropped to his considerable belly and flattened himself, frantically trying to press into the small space. It didn't work. His stomach was too large.

"Oh, hell," Dakota muttered.

The front fender of a red sportscar nosed out past the bank's stucco exterior.

Logan gestured with the muzzle of his pistol. "Get behind it!"

As the SUV maneuvered around two smashed cars in the center of the small intersection, Julio scrambled on his hands and knees for the rear of the Jeep. He crouched, back pressed against the trunk, breathing heavily and clutching that cross like a lifeline. He stared at Logan with wide, terrified eyes.

Logan lifted one finger to his lips. Julio couldn't move or make a sound. If he was discovered, they all were.

Julio gave an almost imperceptible nod of his head.

Logan could just make out Shay's form in the shadows beneath the Jeep. If they were lucky, the passengers in the sportscar would lack the situational awareness and sharp eye required to see what didn't belong.

Maybe it was just a couple of rebellious teens out for a joy ride in the middle of an abandoned city. But Logan wasn't naïve enough to believe that.

The car rumbled toward them.

Logan eased back from the doorway. He ducked below the nearest window, crossed beneath it, and crouched on the opposite side so he could glance through it at an angle while he was still shielded in heavy shadows. Heart racing, he raised the pistol, sighting the car as it came at them, ready to shoot.

It was a bright red Corvette, so shiny it almost hurt to look at it.

The dealer tags and sales decals were still attached. It was definitely stolen, likely from a dealership just outside the localized EMP radius but inside the evacuated hot zone.

The top was down. Four passengers rode inside. They were young, in their teens and early twenties. All Latino, all tattooed, and except for the driver, all carrying assault rifles—an M4 and a couple of AR-15s.

A strong whiff of alcohol and weed reached his nostrils. They cruised slowly, music blasting, both rear passengers checking each side of the road. Raucous laughter echoed in the hot air.

They must be on patrol, either too stupid or too high to care about the radiation. *Keep on driving, just keep driving on through.*

The car zigzagged into the oncoming lane as it swerved to miss the Jeep parked in front of the office building. Shay lay absolutely still beneath the vehicle. Still, if someone looked closely, they'd see her arm, the shape of a leg, a white sneaker.

Julio was on his hands and knees at the rear of the Jeep, bending to peer beneath the undercarriage so he could watch the Corvette approach. It was a smart move, as there was no way for Logan to signal to either Julio or Shay from his vantage point behind the wall.

As the Corvette drew almost even with the front of the Jeep, Julio scrambled backward and edged around the rear bumper on the right, until he was pressed against the rear passenger door facing the sidewalk and the office entrance.

With aching slowness, the Corvette eased out of Logan's line of sight. He strained his ears, listening as the sound of the rumbling engine faded.

He couldn't tell if they'd turned onto another street. He edged farther out and risked a glance out the window. They were fifty yards down the street now. The car had stopped.

The thugs were all facing the front. One of them was pointing at the next traffic light. The two in the rear aimed their rifles and let loose a volley of gunfire. The center traffic light swung wildly, colored glass and metal shards spraying everywhere.

Idiots. They didn't even have ear protection.

Logan glanced back at Julio, who was sweating and pale-faced and looked about ready to have a heart attack right there in the street. He frowned at Logan, giving him a *what the heck do I do now?* look.

Waiting for the thugs to lose interest in target practice and move on before acting appeared to be the best option. If Julio and Shay tried to run for cover now, their movement could draw the hostiles' attention.

On the other hand, if even one bothered to look behind them, they would see Julio crouched on the right side of the Jeep. He was still exposed.

It was less than ten feet from the Jeep to the office building's front door. They could make it. If they were fast enough.

Logan made a split-second decision. It was better to get them both to safety while the gangsters were distracted. Maybe it was the wrong choice, but sometimes indecision was the worst option.

He gestured at Julio with the pistol. "Come on! Move!"

Julio dropped and reached for Shay underneath the Jeep. She seized his hand and he yanked her roughly out from beneath the vehicle.

"I'll get them." Dakota moved back toward the shattered front door.

Hunched and bent double to stay low, Shay and Julio hobbled over the sidewalk. Dakota took one step outside the doorway and grabbed Shay's other arm, dragging them in.

As soon as she was a few feet inside, Shay leaned against the nearest wall, breathing hard. Dust and gravel clung to her legs, stomach, and arms. She brushed it off frantically. "Did they see us?"

Logan didn't take his eyes off the Corvette. "No, I don't think so."

The music switched off.

Abruptly, the only sound was the idling engine.

"What are they doing?" Dakota hissed.

Logan held up one finger.

The tension wound tighter and tighter. He felt it in his chest, his guts. They stared at each other, eyes wide and white in the shadows.

He counted the seconds in his head. Had they been seen? What the hell were the gangsters up to?

Then came the sound of wheels crunching and crackling over the debris in the road.

They were coming back.

13

LOGAN

The thugs were coming back. Which meant they were in serious trouble.

Logan wasn't a match for three semi-automatic assault rifles. Not with his 9mm pistol and four measly bullets.

Not with Shay wounded and unable to run.

You could run. He glanced down at his Glock. He could escape easily. He knew how to be soundless. He had the speed and the endurance to flee out the back before these scumbags even hauled themselves out of their sweet ride.

You don't owe these people anything. Why was he even here? Because a pretty girl had begged him for help? Because of a ludicrous promise of safety and endless booze in some cabin in the middle of the world's biggest swamp?

He was out of his mind. The blast had shaken loose some core, elemental part of him and reset everything backward and upside down.

Three days ago, he'd had his head buried in a bottle, sleepwalking through his days as a forklift operator, mildly disappointed each day he awoke and found himself still breathing.

Now he was considering who he could stab in the back to get himself out alive.

A shrink couldn't untangle that level of crazy. There wasn't time for navel-gazing, anyway.

He wanted to live. If it came down to it, he wasn't putting himself in danger for the waitress or anyone else. He was willing to leave them behind.

"Take them and go—look for a back exit," Logan whispered to Dakota. "I'll follow. You need the head start with Shay."

Julio put his arm around Shay and hurried after Dakota into the darkened bowels of the building. Logan returned his attention to the hostiles outside.

The Corvette stopped parallel to the Jeep. The engine switched off. Three of the thugs piled out of the car; the driver remained inside. Their bronze skin was red and patchy, like they'd been exposed to an awful sunburn. Or radiation.

"What'd you think you saw?" one of them asked, a skinny kid of sixteen or seventeen with big jughead ears.

"Here," the second one said, taller but just as skinny, with a du-rag and a giant tattoo of a tiger spread across his shoulder and chest beneath his white tank top.

He strode over to the wrought-iron table Dakota and the others had been sitting at not five minutes before. "Took me a minute to figure out what my brain was tryin' to tell me. This table wasn't like this on our last roll through here this mornin', all pretty like. There ain't no dust or ash on it at all. And lookie here." He picked something up off the table.

Logan sucked in his breath. One of Shay's gum wrappers from the package he'd brought her. Stupid, stupid, stupid.

"You think it might be them?" one of them asked.

"What're you waiting for? Go get 'em," the driver said.

"They're probably long gone already," the kid whined. "It's hot as hell out here. I feel worse than sh—"

"And you look it, too," the driver growled. "You heard Salvador. We're cleanin' this place up. This is Blood Outlaw territory now. No one steals from us or murders one of our own. No one."

"We'll find them," Tiger Tattoo said. "They'll pay for what they did to Potillo."

Logan's heartrate increased. The thug in Old Navy had been found. Or the escaped snitch had told his tale. Either way, the Blood Outlaws were searching for them.

"And if it's La Raza or the Syndicate?" the kid asked, mentioning two other well-known gangs with strongholds in Miami.

Tiger Tattoo smiled, revealing a row of gold teeth. "We'll take care of them, too."

"Spread out," the driver ordered. "Two and two. You two take that side, we'll take this one."

Two of them started across the street, assault rifles in hand, short-wave radios attached to their low-slung belts.

Logan melted back into the shadows and moved swiftly and silently across the foyer. The front room was some kind of sitting area featuring padded chairs with a sickly green palm tree pattern from the nineties mixed with shiny brass coffee tables displaying dusty *Human Resources Digest* magazines.

There was a welcome counter surrounded by toppled potted palms to the right, a water cooler and coffee station below a splintered giant mirror to the left, and a set of double doors straight ahead next to the elevators and emergency stairwell.

He didn't want to head to the second or third stories. It cut off their options for escape. Better to stay on the first floor. He hoped Dakota was smart enough to do the same.

He pushed through the double doors to find a huge open area cluttered with cubicles stuffed with computer equipment and personal mementos, golf mugs, and family photos. Large offices for the bigwigs lined either side of the large room, placards announcing each name and title affixed to the faux wooden doors.

He blinked to adjust his eyes. Daylight filtered through the opened doors of several offices large enough for exterior windows. The interior was still deeply shadowed, but there was enough light to see by.

This was his chance. He should go for one of the offices, vault through the shattered window, and make a run for it on his own...

Noises reached him from the foyer. Voices. Something banging. Maybe the water cooler being knocked over just for the hell of it.

He spotted Dakota at the far end of the cubicle maze, peeking her head out of a narrow door, searching for him. When she caught sight of him, she widened her eyes and gestured silently at him. *Come on.*

His brain told him to run for the window. Get out while he still could. Wash his hands of this whole mess, these people he hardly knew and sure as hell wasn't responsible for.

But something else made him hesitate, something he couldn't explain even to himself. He should run—but he didn't.

Before he could talk himself out of it, he ducked below the level of the cubicles and sprinted, half-bent, toward Dakota and the others.

He passed a break room on the left and glimpsed a few round tables, a compact fridge, and several vending machines. It was a good thing Dakota was smart enough not to hide in there. The thugs would probably make a beeline for it.

More sounds from the foyer. Closer now.

His pulse roaring in his head, he reached the door labeled 'utility closet' and slipped inside. He blinked, but it was too dark to see.

"Shut the door!" Dakota hissed.

He pulled on the brass handle, attempting to close the latch as soundlessly as possible, but the door stuck two inches before closing. He yanked harder. No give. Something was blocking it.

The Glock still in his right hand, he fumbled with his left, feeling metal shelving, bottles of cleaner and bleach, industrial-sized rolls of paper towels. A wooden mop handle. The thick fibers of the mop must be trapped beneath the door or in the hinge—

The double doors burst open, followed by a cacophony of loud voices.

Logan stiffened. There was no time to move the mop out of the way or make even the smallest noise.

He glanced behind him. His eyes more adjusted now, he could barely make out a long, narrow room about seven feet by fourteen feet lined with metal shelves sticking out perpendicular to the wall. On the left, halfway in, Dakota, Shay, and Julio huddled behind three large, wheeled trash bins.

Everyone was frozen, crouched and terrified, waiting for whatever was going to happen next. The only thing standing between them and two hostiles with AR-15s was a flimsy hollow-core faux wood door that wasn't even closed all the way, let alone locked.

There was no room behind the trash cans for him to hide. The shelving might provide enough camouflage, but if he attempted to move now, he might accidentally trip or knock something over and expose them all.

The only thing Logan had going for him was the element of surprise. He sank silently into a defensive crouch, gun up, a bullet already in the chamber, and waited.

14

LOGAN

Through the crack in the door, Logan watched the two gangsters make their way deeper into the interior of the room.

The first guy was in his early twenties. He was barrel-chested with a square head and blocky features--a wide face and forehead, broad cheekbone, flat nose. The second one was the kid with the big ears. He took the right side closest to the utility door.

They both moved slowly. The kid hunched like he was in pain. Squarehead breathed so heavily Logan could hear him panting from thirty feet away. He kept pausing to mop his damp forehead with a red handkerchief.

Squarehead banged the muzzle of the AR-15 against several of the cubicle walls. "Come out, come out, wherever you are..." He paused to hack up something and spat it out on the carpet.

The kid wandered down the far aisle. He glanced half-heartedly into each cubicle, ignoring the offices completely. He scanned the break room and made a face, as if the sight of food made him ill.

Logan watch him shuffle closer and closer. He stopped at the last cubicle, not four feet away.

The kid slumped into one of the padded, ergonomic office chairs and leaned his head back. With a sigh, he opened a drawer and banged it shut. He dumped a sheaf of papers from a rack and tossed them around on the floor. He knocked the computer off the desk with a thump.

Whether he was simply too sick, bored, or lazy, his heart wasn't in the hunt.

Abruptly, the kid bent and heaved into a trash can. The sound of vomit splattered against plastic. He straightened with a groan, holding his stomach, the AR-15 swinging freely on its sling.

Radiation sickness, then. At least something might go right for them, after all. Logan shifted slightly, just enough to support his gun hand on his knee. Whatever happened, he was ready.

"Screw this." The kid wiped his mouth with his forearm. "I'm outta here. Salvador can bag his own damn goons. They're ghosts, man."

"Don't let the Spider hear you talkin' like that," Squarehead snapped from across the room.

The kid stood and swayed a little. "He said if there weren't no ash, there ain't no radioactive poison or whatever. Then why do I feel like this, man? Like my insides are turning out? Got this damn headache, too."

Squarehead shrugged and picked at one of the blisters forming at the corner of his mouth. "Stop talkin'. You're just making it worse. You clear your side?"

The kid kicked the trash can. It rolled across the carpet and bumped against the utility closet door, spewing its contents. The stench of vomit filled Logan's nostrils. He clamped his mouth shut and stopped breathing.

The kid stood less than three feet away from him. Through the crack in the door, Logan sighted his shoulder, adjusted the gun a fraction higher, and aimed at one oversized ear.

He could take out this one easily enough, but Squarehead and his AR-15 would be trouble. And once they heard the shots, the others would come running. *Don't make me do this. Just walk away.*

The kid barely glanced at the offices or the utility door right in front of him. He looked at the stairs for a moment, then turned away. "Yeah. All clear."

"Let's roll. This place is like a sauna."

Their voices faded as they exited the building.

Logan and the others listened, unmoving, until the Corvette roared back to life and the car rumbled slowly down the road. Finally, the sounds faded completely. The eerie silence returned.

"That was too close," Dakota said as she untangled her limbs and rose to her feet.

"Thank God we're okay," Julio said, letting out a shaky breath. "I nearly peed my pants."

"Good thing you didn't." Shay patted his arm with a gentle smile. "Thank goodness for gangbangers with a poor work ethic, I guess."

Dakota wrinkled her nose. "What's that awful smell?"

"You don't want to know." Logan pushed open the door and stepped into the room. "Let's get out of here before they decide to come back."

They hurried past the cubicles, the offices, and the break room. No one felt like pausing to stock up. They pushed through the double doors and entered the foyer.

A scuffling sound came from the right. Beside the elevators, the door to the emergency stairwell swung open.

Logan whipped around, his pistol already out and pointed at the threat.

15

DAKOTA

"Please—don't shoot," a man said as he thrust both hands in the air. "I'm unarmed. I'm not here to hurt anyone."

"Then who are you?" Dakota asked.

"I—I work here. In accounting," he stammered nervously. He pointed up at the ceiling with one shaking finger. "My name is Dave. Dave Spangler. A handful of my co-workers are still upstairs. We're sheltering in place. You know...from the bomb."

Dave Spangler was a middle-aged, balding white guy with a bristly mustache and heavy jowls, his gut swelling over his creased khaki pants. He looked exactly like she imagined all accountants did.

Logan lowered his pistol so it wasn't pointed at the guy's chest, but he remained fully in alert mode. So was Dakota. Her heart was still hammering against her ribs from the near miss with the Blood Outlaws.

"We just wanted to make contact with the outside world, to talk to another person, you know?" Dave said.

"We know," Julio said kindly. "Don't worry, we're not dangerous."

"Speak for yourself," Logan muttered

"How many people are here with you?" Dakota asked.

"T-twelve," Dave said. "We've been holed up in here since the blast. The first emergency broadcasts told us to evacuate, but I've read a few novels about potential nuclear attacks. It was science fiction, of course, but everything it said about sheltering in place made sense, you know? Most of our co-workers fled. We've stayed upstairs in an inner conference room."

"Smart choice," Dakota said.

"The others didn't want me to come down to talk to you. But I know you're not like those gangs. We watched what happened from one of the second-story windows. Those scumbags came after you. You're lucky they gave up so quickly. The things we've heard..."

He shook his head, looking ill. "People are already rioting and looting. We can hear them at night. Screaming and gunshots. Gangs are taking advantage of the power vacuum, I guess. They're fighting each other for territory. We can hear them ransacking stores, banks, pharmacies, you name it. Haven't seen a police car or heard a siren since it started the first night."

"Who's doing this?" Dakota asked, her gut tightening. She already had a good guess.

"The worst are the ones that call themselves Blood Outlaws. They've been a growing crime problem for years, but the governor never could contain them. Now, they're trying to control the remaining food and whatever else they think is valuable, patrolling the streets like the police. They're killing rival gang members or anyone who tries to resist them."

Dakota repressed a shudder. It already seemed like another lifetime, but the attack at Old Navy had happened only hours ago.

She was already concerned enough about Maddox and whatever other random psychos were roaming the city. Now the Blood Outlaws were hunting them, too.

Uneasiness swept through her. This wasn't going to be the worst of it, not by a long shot.

"May I put my hands down, now?" Dave asked nervously.

"No," Logan said, at the same time Shay exclaimed, "Of course!"

Dave looked confused. Dakota rolled her eyes. "Go ahead."

Dave turned to the stairwell. "You can come down now."

Behind him, a petite Haitian woman in her fifties with silver cropped hair and a younger Asian woman in a wrinkled business suit and smeared eye-makeup cautiously descended the stairs. "This is Lydie—" he gestured at the older black woman, "and Amy."

Both women nodded tightly.

"Can you tell us anything?" Dakota asked. "We haven't met anyone else, either." Anyone else alive, she meant, but she didn't say the words out loud.

"None of our computers or electronics work," Lydie said, "but Amy has this portable radio she brings in to play oldies at lunchtime...it still works. The batteries are about to die, so we're conserving it now. They play the same emergency broadcast on every station over and over, but once in a while, they add new information."

Dakota and Logan exchanged tense glances. Finally, they were about to get real information.

"We only know what we heard on the news before the blast," Logan said. "What the hell happened?"

Dave and Amy only shook their heads. Lydie's mouth pressed into a grim line. "It's so awful...Thirteen. There were thirteen."

"Thirteen what?" Shay asked.

"Bombs," Amy whispered. "Thirteen Improvised Nuclear Devices detonated across the United States."

Shay made a wounded sound in the back of her throat. Logan sucked in a sharp, startled breath.

All the blood rushed to Dakota's head. She felt dazed, shaken to her core.

Thirteen cities decimated just like Miami. It was almost unbelievable. Someone's idea of a sick joke. Except that they'd survived one of the blasts. They knew it was all too real.

"Mother Mary and Joseph." Julio touched his gold cross, his pallor ashen.

"There were supposed to be fourteen," Dave said, "but the one in Chicago was discovered and defused in time."

"Which cities?" Logan asked hoarsely.

Lydie recited them like they'd been burned into her mind. "Miami. Los Angeles. Long Beach. Charleston. Norfolk. Savannah. New Orleans. Houston. Corpus Christi. Seattle. New York City. Atlanta. And Washington D.C."

Dakota stared at the woman, barely able to comprehend her words. There was something about the targeted cities, something that didn't make sense. But before she could ask, Dave was talking again.

"The terrorist bastards managed to get the IND close enough to wipe out the White House, the Capitol Building, the Supreme Court. Only nine Congress members are still alive. The president and vice-president didn't make it."

Lydie sucked in a harsh breath. "President Pro Tempore of the Senate Dianna Harrington is now the president of the United States. I didn't even know who she was before two days ago. And now she's president."

Even after all they'd suffered, the survivors' words still struck her like a physical blow. It was worse than she'd thought. Far worse.

Hadn't Ezra warned her of this?

Another memory niggled at the far edges of her mind. Raving, pulpit-pounding sermons of impending doom, dire predictions of fury and fire descending from the heavens to scorch the earth and every person in it—everyone but the chosen.

She shook the memory out of her head. Those were the delusions of a madman and the mindless fools brainwashed into worshiping his depraved teachings.

She'd left all that behind the night she'd fled the compound.

She never wanted to think of the Prophet or any of his damn Shepherds again.

"How many people—" Julio swallowed. Tears shimmered in his eyes. He didn't bother to wipe them away. "How many dead?"

Lydie closed her eyes and spoke like she was reciting from a news report she'd memorized. Maybe she had. Maybe facts and figures with such terrible arithmetic were seared into your mind forever.

"The emergency broadcasts reported over 100,000 people are dead in New York City alone, with 200,000 seriously injured. Washington D.C. is reporting 300,000 injuries. And that doesn't even include all the people suffering from radiation. They don't know how many people are sick—or will be soon.

"The news estimated at least a million people are already dead," Lydie said heavily. "Millions injured. Even more sick with radiation. Every hospital in the country is just overwhelmed."

"What about Miami itself?" Dakota asked.

"It looks like a war zone," Amy said. Her voice was so soft, Dakota could barely hear her. Shadows rimmed her blood-shot eyes. Her expression was haunted. "Ground zero is the iconic Miami Tower. It no longer exists. The business district is gone. The Miami skyline has just been...decimated. Miami Center, the Met 2, the Southeast Financial Center building, Vizcayne, the Asia..."

Shay gnawed on her thumbnail, silently shaking her head, as if her disbelief could somehow stop the endless stream of horror.

But it couldn't. There was no stopping any of it.

It felt like a terrible nightmare.

A chance of geography had spared them from the worst of it—the collapsing skyscrapers, horrific third-degree burns, and doses of radiation high enough to kill a grown man within days.

Dakota had never thought herself lucky before now; today, she counted herself blessed. Yet even in her relief, guilt speared her.

Why her? Why them? They weren't any more deserving than anyone else.

It was all random, accidental and arbitrary. Who lived or died determined by nothing more than a cosmic roll of the dice.

The thought chilled her to the bone.

Shay and Julio talked with the group for another minute, but Dakota hardly heard them. More than ever, she wanted to get the hell out of there.

She caught Logan's gaze. He nodded.

"What're your plans?" Julio asked.

"We're staying for another day or two." Dave ran a shaky hand through his thinning hair. "We have food and water from the break room. Then we'll head north on I-95 until we find help or a FEMA camp for all the evacuees and start searching for our families."

Shay hugged Lydie and Amy. Julio shook Dave's hand. Even Dakota felt a strange connection to these strangers. They were all survivors of the same devastating catastrophe.

"Thanks for the information," Dakota said. "And good luck."

Within five minutes, they'd left their fellow survivors and Palm Industrial Center behind and were back on the road, headed toward Eden.

16

MADDOX

Maddox shuffled down the center of the torn and buckled road.

He'd had to turn back and find an alternate route after an avalanche of debris had tumbled down between two mid-rise condo buildings, sealing off the main avenue.

It was no matter. A few blocks down, he could turn east and then north again, weaving his way through the rubble and destruction until he found the way cleared for him.

He had faith it would be.

For several hours yesterday, he'd been overwhelmed with weakness from the crash. His ribs ached fiercely. His head and the base of his spine throbbed.

His stomach still felt like it had been turned inside out.

He hadn't eaten in two days. He wasn't hungry.

Maybe he was experiencing some of the effects of radiation. Back in the tunnel, he'd blacked out for hours, which had protected him from the prompt radiation at detonation.

But maybe there was more out here.

When night fell, he'd been forced to take shelter inside a hotel lobby. It hadn't been easy to find one free of fetid, rotting bodies, but at last he'd succeeded.

He'd sought out a comfortable leather sofa and slept for hours. A water cooler spared from the blast offered the only sustenance he needed.

He longed for that water now. Hot, humid air soaked his shirt with sweat. The blazing heat sapped his strength, but he pressed on.

Ahead of him, a man blocked his path. A man kneeling in the valley of a mountain range of rubble, oily smoke rising up all around him.

Something about the way the man knelt, as if in supplication, gave him pause.

The man looked up at Maddox.

He was naked, his skin a boiling mass of raw burns. His face was scorched so badly that Maddox could see flecks of bone within the wreckage of flesh. His eyes were filmed with milky white—he'd been blinded by the light flash.

"Save me," he begged.

The man longed for death, for an end to his earthly suffering.

The man was a wretch, as were all who refused the call of the Prophet, who chose their own selfish path over The Way. He was a sinner being punished for his sins.

Maddox didn't know what the man had done. He didn't need to know. But he could help the man if he wished.

His Beretta M9 was holstered at his hip. But he didn't have spare ammo; his bag had been left in the taxi, burned to ash or melded to the backseat.

He didn't know what other obstacles lay in his path. He didn't know how difficult the task before him would be—whether the girls would come easily, or if more persuasive force would be required.

He needed every bullet for himself.

Besides, this man was simply enduring the punishment he

deserved. Maybe when he had suffered enough, God would grant him mercy.

But that wasn't up to Maddox.

He didn't care what happened to the man. He didn't care what happened to any of these people. They'd made their choice, just like he had made his.

He sidestepped the wretch, leaving him to his penance.

Maddox continued his journey, every step bringing him closer to his goal, to completing his mission and taking his place as one of the chosen, a true Shepherd.

Fixed always in his mind was the tan stucco house with the powder-blue shutters and the pink flamingo stuck in the mulch.

17

DAKOTA

After they left the office building and Dave, Lydie, and Amy behind, Dakota and the others walked for another hour, forced to backtrack again to avoid more fires. The entire city seemed like it was ablaze.

They kept to side roads and back alleys, always ready to run and hide if they heard another vehicle roaming the streets. It was necessary, though it only slowed them down further.

Dakota felt every wasted second ticking inside her head like another bomb waiting to explode.

No one talked about the thirteen bombs. It was too damn depressing, too overwhelming. The state of the country out there—and the possibility that things might be worse outside of Miami, not better—was too horrifying to contemplate.

At least the groans from the trapped and dying in nearby buildings had faded away. Now, it was silent again but for the occasional buzzing of flies and their own footsteps.

Logan trudged beside her. He swiped sweat from his forehead with his arm and pulled a half-melted Snickers bar out of his bag with one hand, his other hand occupied with a Budweiser.

He'd already had three.

"So, after we get your sister, who's gonna meet us at the end of this road? Your father or grandfather?" he asked. "A crazy prepper uncle?"

He clearly just wanted a distraction. But then, so did she. "I already told you. It's just me and my sister. No family."

"None at all?"

"Other than her, everyone who mattered is dead." Which was true enough.

He took a swig of beer and alternated it with a bite of candy bar. "Who owns this safehouse of yours?"

"A friend."

He cocked his brows. "A friend's gonna share his hard-earned loot with you? With us? Don't know many friends like that. Especially preppers. It's every man for himself."

Ezra would take them back. If she had faith in anything in this world, it was in him.

He'd forgive her. He had to.

"This one will."

"The only preppers I've ever heard of are crazy. Paranoid out of their minds. He like that?"

"It's not paranoia if you're right."

She closed her eyes for a moment, shutting out the desolation around her, the awful reality of smoke and the fire and the death. She thought of the warm and cozy cabin, of Ezra, gruff and grumpy but still a solid, comforting presence, a ray of brightness in the darkness of her memories.

She needed a good memory right now to anchor her, to sustain her. She was desperate for it. She let her mind drift back to that first night.

"You came through the only break in the fence," Ezra had said later, once he'd shown her the booby traps in the yard that they'd miraculously avoided. The storm had knocked the tree into the fence the night before; Ezra had planned to repair it the next day.

The padlock *had* been left open; in her panic, she hadn't even noticed.

Ezra had been in the middle of transferring a few soon-to-expire goods from storage to his pantry when the motion sensor lights flared to life.

He'd watched them on his cameras, Remington Versa Max 12-gauge shotgun in hand, ready and determined to defend his territory, as he had before. As he would again.

Something about them had stayed his hand—maybe because they'd only stolen what they needed, or because Eden was clearly still a child—or maybe their dreary clothing told its own dismal story.

Later, she'd discovered the photographs lining the hallway walls —all taken by his late wife, who'd died four years before of lung cancer.

The photos depicted the wildlife of the 'Glades in their natural habitats: a wild boar snuffling in the dirt; egrets and herons taking flight over an expanse of dark water; a close-up of a bull gator's massive, arrow-shaped head, his jagged-toothed maw hinged open; a hornbill sweeping its bill in the water, trawling for fish; a line of turtles sunning themselves on a moss-covered log; a diamondback rattler slithering through the pinelands.

Maybe it was the drawing that did it—a fragile, tenuous connection between these two desperate strangers and his dead wife.

Whatever his reasons, he'd decided to take them in.

Filled with a jumbled mix of trepidation and relief, Dakota had followed Ezra Burrows into the tin-roofed cabin that was surprisingly well-furnished for a hermit.

To her surprise, he'd laid Eden gently on his cracked leather sofa, mindless of the blood. So exhausted she could barely keep her eyes open, she'd knelt by the sofa, gripping Eden's small hand, and watched as he cleaned and sutured the gash in her sister's throat.

He gave her pills from a strange-looking bottle. He explained they were fish antibiotics, nearly as good as the high-priced stuff pharmaceutical companies sold for hundreds of bucks.

"Soon as she's conscious, you'll be on your way," he growled, the flickering lamplight scoring his wrinkles in shadows deep as canyons.

The days passed. Eden regained consciousness, but her wound became inflamed. She burned with fever, her skin clammy, her eyes glassy and unfocused.

"I'm takin' her to a hospital where she belongs," he said more than once.

Each time, Dakota's abject terror gave him pause.

"Anything but that," she pleaded. "Just fix her. I'll do anything."

His scowl deepened. He never did call an ambulance. If Eden had worsened, he likely would have, but she didn't. Slowly, over several days, Eden began to improve.

In between tending to Eden, Ezra put Dakota to work. She helped peel and boil potatoes and carrots for a nutritious, easy-to-swallow broth.

She weeded his garden bursting with sweet potatoes, bell peppers, lima beans, cherry tomatoes, and okra—her time at the compound had already taught her the difference between plants and weeds—cleaned out the cages in the rabbit warren, and fed the chickens that wandered the property.

Ezra had a good setup. Even though they were in the middle of nowhere, solar panels on the roof supplied electricity. Ezra ran the stove and refrigerator on propane and used a pitcher pump to draw well water, along with several cisterns to collect rain.

A forty-foot antenna near the shed connected him to the rest of the world via ham radio.

On the third afternoon, she discovered the western side of the property. A fishing dock stretched out into the water. Several dozen yards away, paper targets fluttered over a tall stack of hay bales in a makeshift shooting range.

After a dinner of rabbit stew, she worked up the nerve to ask the question burning on her tongue. "Will you teach me to shoot?"

He watched her over the mug of his black coffee with flinty blue eyes. "What for?"

She considered her answer. "So I'm never helpless again."

He set his mug down on the hand-hewn plank table. For a long moment, he was silent, staring down into the dark liquid, a tense, brooding expression on his wizened face.

"How did you get here?" he asked finally.

"There are people," she started, her voice tremulous. If he knew who was after them, he'd kick them out for sure. But she couldn't make herself lie to him. "They might be looking for us."

"How did you get here?" he asked again, his voice hard.

"Airboat. We found the rotted dock and the old cabin—"

He rose without a word, seized his Remington from beside the door, and left.

He didn't return for hours.

She hadn't known where he'd gone until months later, when he finally told her he'd sunk the boat. He'd done it to keep them safe, to keep Maddox and the Shepherds away.

For a while, it had worked.

The next day, he began lessons. He taught her to shoot with his Glock 19 and Remington shotgun, and even his M4 carbine. He showed her how to take down an assailant swiftly and efficiently with a quality tactical knife—taught her to keep it hidden until she was ready to attack, then to lunge in, swift, brutal, and deadly.

After a week, Eden's fever receded. With the infection conquered, the wound slowly healed, leaving a ridged and ragged three-inch scab stretching from two inches below her left ear to the front of her neck.

Her ruined throat would only allow her to make a low rasping sound. Eden could no longer speak.

"Must be her vocal cords got cut," Ezra said, frowning down at her. "A proper doctor—"

Fear slid between Dakota's ribs like a blade. "No!"

It was a terrible choice—a decision between your sister's voice and her soul, possibly her very life. The decision tore at Dakota, shredding her heart with grief, guilt, and regret.

She hated herself for it. But she did not waver.

"No doctors. No hospitals."

Normally a bright, bubbly child, Eden became wan and withdrawn.

In those first weeks, she barely left the cabin. She only communicated through frustrated gestures Dakota couldn't understand.

One day, Ezra left and returned with several notebooks—a couple lined for writing, another that was blank inside, with a cute unicorn leaping over a rainbow emblazoned on its front.

He handed Eden a box of artist-quality colored pencils. "For drawing," he said gruffly. "Don't leave these lying around. Clean up after yourself, or they'll end up in the trash."

He turned without another word and stomped out of the cabin, his Ruger American hunting rifle slung across his shoulder.

Eden waited until he was gone.

She bent her head and wrote quickly, fiercely. She held up the notepad and thrust it at Dakota. *Why are we here? What happened?*

Dakota went rigid. She had put off the question for as long as possible, dreading the answer.

She couldn't bear the thought of the condemnation in Eden's eyes once she knew the truth.

18

DAKOTA

"What do you remember about that night?" Dakota had asked anxiously.

They were in the bedroom Ezra had fashioned for them from his "Ham Shack," the second room that housed all of his amateur radio equipment.

He'd set up two hand-made duck-feather mattresses on the wood plank floor. A scarred wooden dresser sidled against the desk where he kept a radio transceiver, rectangular tuner, old-fashioned headphones, a set of medium-sized speakers, and several other strange machines covered with dials and knobs.

Dakota repeated the question.

Eden only shook her head in confusion.

She didn't remember. She didn't know. She didn't know that Jacob was dead or how Maddox had betrayed them.

She didn't know what Dakota had done.

It was a blessing. Dakota alone would carry the poisonous truth deep inside her. It was Dakota who lived with the regret, the shame.

Only two people alive knew what really happened that night.

Dakota would never forget—her nightmares wouldn't let her.

And neither would Maddox.

"We're safe now," she said. "You're safe. Do you understand?"

Eden scribbled her response on her paper. *I'm not going to the Prophet?*

"You don't belong to him. Not now, not ever."

What about family?

"Something bad happened."

What?

"I'll tell you later, when you're better."

Tell me now.

Dakota shook her head, adamant.

Eden couldn't handle it. She was too sweet, too trusting, too good. The truth would break her.

It was bad enough she knew about the Prophet. She couldn't know how her own family had betrayed her.

"All you need to know is that it's not safe for us there anymore."

Eden thrust the notepad at Dakota. *Why????*

"It's safer for everyone we care about if we don't go back."

Eden frowned and worked her jaw, trying to speak, but only that low, rasping moan escaped. She tore off the sheet of paper, crumpled it in frustration, and hurled it to the floor between their mattresses.

Dakota closed her hands over Eden's. "Do you trust me?"

Eden nodded without hesitation.

"Do you know that I love you?"

She nodded again.

"You are my sister, and I am yours. Do you understand? We're all we have now. We're each other's family." Dakota smoothed out the wrinkled paper and handed it back to her sister. "I need you to be with me in this, okay?"

Eden's eyes filled with tears. *Will it ever be safe to go back?*

"Of course," Dakota lied. "Soon, I promise."

Finally, Eden gave a sad little nod.

Dakota sucked in a steadying breath. "And we need to change our names."

Eden blanched.

"Just the last name. So bad people can't find us, okay? I was thinking Sloane. I knew a girl named Sloane, back before...it has a nice ring to it."

Tears sparked in Eden's blue eyes. *I miss Maddox and Jacob and Father. I miss home.*

Dakota bit back a sharp retort. Someday, she'd tell Eden the truth.

But she was too brainwashed with love and loyalty to see it now, to understand how they'd treated her like chattel, no better than a slave to be sold at auction.

These were the things Dakota never worked up the courage to tell Ezra.

And yet, the way he looked at them sometimes—not with pity but with an awareness, a dark understanding—though he kept them to himself, she knew he had his suspicions. Suspicions confirmed the day he saw her scars.

Nine days into their stay, with Dakota still sleeping with one wary eye open and Eden barely coherent, Dakota helped mend the electrified, barbed wire fencing damaged in the storm.

As she struggled to pull up a strand of damaged wire caught on a tree branch, she accidentally stepped into a gopher tortoise burrow. Her ankle twisted painfully, and she fell against the barbed wire.

She jerked away but not quickly enough, tearing a large, jagged rip in the back of her shirt. The hot breeze brushed against her exposed skin.

Her breath snagged in her throat. She went completely still.

The torn fabric revealed the neat rows of circular scars spanning her back. She didn't have to see them herself to know what they looked like.

From the wings of her shoulder blades down to her lower spine, she'd been branded dozens of times. Some were years old, now a puckered, shiny pink; others were fresh, savage red welts.

Shame spread fire-hot beneath her skin. "Please, I can explain. I'm clumsy and—"

Ezra had been looking at her, but at her words, he turned sharply away. She stared at his broad shoulders, too stunned to finish her sentence.

"Expect you'll be needing another shirt," he said. "Back at the house, you'll find one of mine on the line."

He never asked where they came from or who'd done it. That night, she found a jar of burn ointment on her nightstand.

The next morning, Ezra left early in his F-250 pickup and returned before breakfast with two five-packs of boys' T-shirts, a few pairs of boys' cargo pants a size too large, and two belts. The belt held the pants up just fine.

"I expect you should be in school," he said when she came out in the new clothes, still pulling at the tags. "There's somewhere better for two girls to be than here."

He reminded her of a bald cypress tree, tall and ancient and strong. He was brusque, but not cruel. Instinctively, she knew he was different from the other men she knew.

He didn't want anything of them, only expected Dakota to help around the property, which she was happy to do. She'd always liked working with her hands, building and feeding and fixing things.

Eden was still sick, but she was getting better under his care.

Dakota liked this place, liked him.

She could breathe here.

"No," she said. "There isn't."

He just looked at her.

"We were homeschooled at the compound."

He raised his gnarled gray eyebrows.

"You can order textbooks online, and Amazon will deliver them straight to your door. Or a post office box," she said quickly at the look of alarm on his face.

"Is that so."

"And tampons."

It was the only time she ever saw him blush.

And that was how they had spent the next eight months: tending the property, harvesting, hunting, cooking, and practicing preps, interspersed with shooting and self-defense lessons. Eden learned how to express herself through her notebook, hand gestures, clicks of her tongue and whistles.

Evenings had been spent around a campfire or the plank table in the kitchen, Eden drawing and Ezra cleaning his guns, Dakota listening raptly as Ezra jawed about his favorite topic—preparing for the impending end of civilization as everyone knew it.

For the first time since her parents had died, Dakota was truly happy.

19

DAKOTA

Dakota blinked and pulled herself out of her reverie. Logan was looking at her sideways. He'd asked her a question she hadn't heard.

"What?"

Logan took another swig of beer and tossed the empty bottle to the street in front of a pale yellow stucco house. As they traveled farther northwest, laundromats, hair salons, and convenience stores slowly gave way to residential areas.

He raked his left hand through his scruffy black hair, several heat-damp strands sticking to his forehead. "I asked what your prepper friend is like."

"Quiet. Scrupulously clean. Good with his hands. And grumpy," she said fondly. "Ezra isn't much for talking unless it's about preparing for the end of the world. He's the one who taught me about EMPs and radiation, how to use a gun, how to survive."

"How'd he learn all that stuff?"

She remembered the dusty medals she'd found in a drawer one day, along with a framed photo of a much younger Ezra Burrows in a sharp, pressed military uniform adorned with ribbons, pins, and medals. He'd been standing next to some sort of major or general. They were both smiling in the photo, but when she'd asked him about it, he'd said, "The past is the past for a reason, girl."

"He was in the Marine Corp, I think. Served in Vietnam. I don't know much more than that. He would never tell me."

"Maybe his PTSD turned into paranoia," Logan said as they sidestepped a mangled SUV that had plowed onto the sidewalk and buried its nose into the front of an apartment complex. "You really never thought he was crazy? Not even a little?"

"Never."

She hadn't thought Ezra was crazy for even a second. She'd admired him. She wanted to be him.

He'd turned his back on the life he didn't want and forged one he did. He was ready for anything.

Except that the one thing he couldn't plan and prepare for was the thing that took what mattered most...his wife.

That same fear dogged her every waking moment and haunted her dreams.

No matter how strong she was, no matter how tough and skilled with a blade and a gun, no matter how many bug out bags she prepped or how often she practiced at the range, no matter how many escape routes and contingency plans she mapped out and memorized—no one could control chaos.

"It's not crazy to think about what bad things might happen." She hesitated. "The world ends for individuals all the time, in a hundred different ways."

Her world had ended the first time when her parents died.

Her Aunt Ada had reluctantly taken her in, forcing her into the strange, awful world of the River Grass Compound—where religion was the new law and the outside ceased to exist, where they smiled bright perfect smiles and quoted Bible verses while they beat you senseless.

Her world ended the second time in the mercy room, standing bloodied and stunned over the body, Eden a collapsed heap beside her.

She'd known the only way forward was to run—to run and run and never look back.

And then a third time when social services forcibly ripped Eden from her arms and sent her to one horrible group home after another, where she fought with fists and teeth and nails to establish a place for herself, sleeping with a shiv beneath her pillow to ensure no asshole ever touched her again.

Her hand strayed to the comfort of the knife at her side. "It's those people who trust a corrupted, broken system that they *know* is broken to take care of them that are the real crazy."

Logan drained his beer and tossed the bottle aside. It landed without breaking and rolled into a gutter. "You might have a point there."

"Everything is more fragile than we want to believe it is. Those people who are prepared? They're the smart ones."

If she'd been prepared, she could have saved Eden sooner. If she'd been prepared, Eden wouldn't have lost her voice and nearly her life.

Dakota wouldn't have the scars disfiguring her back.

And if she'd been prepared, Dakota and Eden wouldn't be separated right now. That failure, at least, she was about to rectify.

She pointed to a dented street sign fifty feet ahead of them. "Bay Point Drive. We're only a bit more than a half a mile away now."

Her heartbeat quickened. She walked faster. Anticipation thrummed through her veins. Almost there. After everything, she was finally just minutes away from rescuing her sister.

Logan nodded. "Let's pick up the pace—"

A scream shattered the humid air. Dakota and Logan both tensed, already reaching for their weapons.

This scream wasn't like the others.

It wasn't low and rasping or full of suffering.

It was loud, piercing, terrified—and close.

20

EDEN

Eden's throat burned with thirst. Her mouth felt stuffed with cotton, her tongue thick and swollen.

When nightmares weren't stalking her, she dreamed of waterfalls, sprinklers, and streams bubbling with clear, cold water.

She lay on her back in the tub on top of the cushions, her knees drawn up. Sometimes she curled onto her side or flopped onto her stomach, searching for a more comfortable position.

But comfort eluded her.

Her lips were dry and cracked. Sour sweat beaded her forehead and dripped down her neck. Her empty stomach gnawed at her insides.

She'd had to use the bathroom a few times that first day, and now the stink hung heavily in the hot and stifling air.

For a long time, Eden stared up toward the ceiling, breathing shallowly, her pulse thumping in time with the fear throbbing through her. The hours passed in a slow daze.

She blinked her gritty eyes and forced them to remain open, even though she couldn't see anything. She didn't want to sleep; the nightmares always found her.

She desperately needed a distraction to keep the terror at bay.

She fumbled around, feeling the side of the tub beneath the cushion until she found her pencil, and opened her notepad to the next page, which she knew was blank. The previous page contained her ASL alphabet drawings.

She began to sketch without really thinking. It didn't matter that she couldn't see. She just needed to do *something*.

After a few strokes, she felt the cypress trees coming to life beneath her fingers, and she knew what she was creating.

The long, rectangular concrete buildings, the clearing with the chickens and the raised gardens, the greenhouses and hydroponic farm, the large kitchen and cafeteria where she'd spent so much of her time learning to cook.

The compound slowly took shape on the page. She couldn't see the pencil or the paper, but she imagined the sun overhead, a great blue heron swooping low over the fishing and airboat docks on the western end of the property.

She drew the classroom with old-fashioned wooden desks and attached metal chairs, colorful science posters on the walls, spelling words of the week laminated and tacked to a spring green bulletin board.

And then the big grassy open area in the compound's center rimmed by picnic tables painted bright pink and blue and yellow. She had loved to sit by the giant fire pit surrounded by Adirondack chairs.

There were the clotheslines strung between the stubby pines, the women hand-washing and hanging the linens; sheets, towels, and long skirts fluttering in the breeze like kites.

To the east, on a raised bump of land, loomed the church—with its hard wooden pews, cement block walls, and the plain but heavy cross hanging behind the imposing pulpit.

She'd spent much of her time there, too. Listening to three-hour sermons four times a week. Preparing herself in purity and obedience to the Prophet. Praying for blessings, for mercy and forgiveness.

Guilt pricked her. She hadn't prayed enough. Not then, and not now.

She didn't draw the collection of off-limits buildings hidden behind a cluster of cypress trees located far back from the rest of the compound. She had never been allowed anywhere near them. None of the women were.

Only the chosen Shepherds of Mercy went back there, men with uniforms and guns and other things she didn't know the names of.

Her father had told her the most holy work of the Prophet took place within those buildings, just like the holy places of the sanctuary in the Old Testament.

She had never understood it, but it wasn't her place to understand such things.

Eden also left out a drawing of the mercy room.

Her heartbeat quickened simply thinking about it. She'd never been allowed inside—but she'd seen Dakota's burns afterward. And what they did to the others, the guilty ones.

Her father always said punishment was merciful. It saved the soul from eternal hellfire. Wasn't that preferred to a little pain on earth?

Eden touched the scar on her throat.

Something bad had happened there. That's what Dakota said. Something so terrible that they couldn't go back.

She didn't remember the event itself—only waking up afterward on a stranger's sofa in a strange cabin, bleary and disoriented, her throat seared with agony, her voice gone.

Whenever she tried to think back to that night, dread clutched her mind in its steel talons, filling her with a rush of hollow terror.

Trying to remember felt like staring into a vast, bottomless black pit.

If you summoned the courage to leap in, to swim down deep— oily darkness sucking at your arms and legs, worming into your ears, your eyes, your mouth—you'd eventually reach that vital, pulsing heart that contained every memory, bright and dark, good and terrible.

It was dangerous, that place where answers were found. Where memory was treacherous. Where the answers you got weren't always the ones you were looking for.

Where the monsters and demons were real.

Dakota told her it was a mercy that she didn't remember. That she didn't *want* to remember. That it was better to forget everything that had come before their time at Ezra's.

But Eden couldn't forget her father or her brothers—not Jacob's easy laugh or the way Maddox could make her feel like the only little girl in the world.

No matter what her memory was hiding from her, she couldn't forget that she still had a family out there.

She wasn't worried about them. She knew they were safe.

The Prophet had promised the faithful would be spared.

Now though, as she licked her cracked lips and tasted blood, she began to worry for herself.

21

DAKOTA

Dakota tensed, instantly on alert. "What was that?"

Beside her, Logan stiffened. He slid his flask into his back pocket, pulled his Glock and held it in the low ready position. "It's just ahead, around the corner of that coffee shop."

"It's someone needing help?" Shay whispered it like a question.

"We'll see."

More voices echoed in the still air. Tense, angry. One, a female voice, was pleading. The hairs on Dakota's neck stood on end.

Maybe they should backtrack and give whatever this was a wide berth. Or maybe this was a chance to make at least one thing right in this horrible, upside-down hell.

Either way, they needed to know what kind of trouble might lay ahead.

"I'll check it out," Logan said.

His hands tremored ever so slightly. It was hardly noticeable, but she caught it. She knew the signs. The alcohol was getting to him. If he wasn't already drunk, he was close.

There was no way in hell she was leaving this up to him. "I'm coming with you. Shay and Julio, find shelter and stay here, just in case."

"Be careful," Julio called softly after them.

He helped Shay ease down along the curb behind a vehicle parked at a 45-degree angle, half on the street, half on the sidewalk. It was an old, burnt husk of a car; only the trunk remained a pristine, glossy pumpkin orange.

Julio touched its side reverently. "A classic 1968 Pontiac Firebird. I restored one like this a few years ago. Such a shame to see it like this."

Another scream rent the air.

"You sure you got this?" Dakota asked Logan doubtfully.

"I'm fine," he muttered and stalked past her.

She didn't believe that for a hot second.

Dakota removed her shoulder bag and lowered the scarf around her neck. Logan followed suit. Together, they moved slowly and carefully around the corner of the coffee shop.

They paused, keeping most of their bodies hidden behind the brick façade, and took in the scene. The air was hazy with smoke. Somewhere beyond their line of sight, more fires burned furiously.

Sixty feet ahead and to their left stood a sagging gas station, the entire right side of the roof collapsed in on itself. Five people crowded around one of the still-upright poles.

They were filthy with dust and soot. The bare skin of their faces, arms, and legs were deep red, like they'd been badly sunburned. Some were pocked with blisters as large as tennis balls.

They wielded improvised weapons—jagged spears of torn rebar, tire irons, a kitchen knife. One Hispanic man, short and stocky but muscular as a boulder beneath his torn and blackened tank top, carried a pistol.

Two people dressed in PPE suits were backed against the pole, their hands up defensively, trying to ward off the impending attack.

Dakota couldn't make out any identifying characteristics through their safety goggles and respirator masks, but the taller one held a medical kit and wore a backpack over one shoulder. A wheeled stretcher stood next to the second, shorter one.

First responders.

"Give us what's ours and you're free to go," said one of the aggressors—a fat Caucasian man in a too-tight Hawaiian shirt with bloodied cuts all over his body. He gripped a large butcher knife.

"They've left us here to die!" spat another Hispanic guy in his late twenties, a red bandanna tied around his head. Burns maimed the entire right side of his torso and tattooed upper arm, his T-shirt hanging in ragged tatters.

He paused to hack up yellow-tinged spittle and blood. He held a three-foot length of twisted rebar in his right hand.

"We're American citizens!" Hawaii snarled. "We have rights!"

In the quiet of a city devoid of car engines, horns, rumbling construction machinery, and the hum of humanity, Dakota and Logan could hear every word clear as day.

"You can't treat us like this, man," Hawaii said. "We paid for those ambulances and fire trucks with our tax dollars. I don't see a single one anywhere!"

"We're here to help," said one of the first responders, the taller, heavier one—a woman. "Others are coming behind us. I'm out of supplies, but I'll go back for more and return."

"We've set up a field hospital a mile west of here," the second responder—a guy—said. "It's just outside the hot zone at Miami Jordan High School off 36th street. You're all mobile. Come with us."

He pointed at the leg of one of the aggressors. "We've even got an extra stretcher for that thigh wound."

A burly black man in a gray pinstriped suit limped closer to the responders. A hunk of twisted metal jutted from his left thigh. He held a pair of tire irons in each hand.

"My wife was trapped in our Toyota," he said, wincing. "She was crushed between a bus and a damn SUV. Where were you then? Huh?"

"We'll come back and help her—"

"She's dead," Pinstripe said, his features contorting with grief. "We waited two days for you people, and you never came."

"I'm sorry for your—" the woman started.

"Too little, too late." His eyes hardened. "You left her out here to die. Just like Hurricane Katrina. Only the rich are worth saving, is that it?"

"Of course not!" the woman said, sounding affronted.

"We've been searching for people for over twenty-five hours," the male responder said. "We couldn't get in until the radiation levels fell—"

"But you could leave all of us out here to be poisoned?" Bandanna scowled. He gestured with the rebar at their suits and masks. "While you have all the protection you need? That doesn't seem fair, does it?"

"Dude, we're doing everything we can," the male responder said. "Come to the high school. We'll get you hooked up with water, a hot meal, and medicine to help with those burns. You'll feel like a new person, I promise you."

Even in his PPE suit, Dakota could tell the male responder was shorter and thinner than his partner. Straight black hair stuck out above the rim of his goggles. His right leg jittered nervously.

"You promise? I think we've had our fill of government *promises*," the guy in the black tank top spat.

Dakota's heart banged against her ribs as she watched. Adrenaline spiked through her veins. This situation was going sideways fast.

"You got food in that pack?" A white woman in her twenties with cropped wheat-blonde hair stained crimson kept wiping blood from her eyes. An ugly, weeping gash arced across her right temple all the way to her chin.

Both of her ears, her nose, and her upper lip were studded with several silver hoops. Her bare, heavily tattooed arms were red and blistered. "How about pain meds?"

"We ran out, but we'll get more—" the female responder started.

Blondie waved a tire iron aggressively at the woman. "You holding out on us? Keeping it all for yourself?"

"We have work to do," the female responder said evenly, though her voice was shaky. "I think it's time for us to go."

"We're just talking," Hawaii said. "That's all. Just asking some pertinent questions of our government representatives. We have a right to know why you're failing so utterly."

Tank Top grunted an affirmative.

Bandanna took a menacing step toward them. "Maybe you should strip off that fancy suit and give it to someone who can actually use it."

"That's a hard pass." The male responder shook his head emphatically. "Harlow's not touching that suit. You people are taking a ride on the crazy train."

"Take it off," Bandanna said in a low, threatening voice. "Now."

"Okay," the woman said, her hands up, trying to placate them. "Just remain calm. We'll do what you ask. We can work this out—"

"No way." The male responder stepped in front of the woman, keeping himself between her and the aggressors. "Dude, you're already almost out of the hot zone. Don't lose your sh—"

"Excuse me?" Bandanna stalked closer. He was less than ten feet away from the responders now. His lip curled in a vicious sneer. "What the hell did you just say to me?"

22

DAKOTA

Dakota watched in tense silence as the group slowly closed in around the first responders. She had hoped the altercation would play itself out without escalating, but it didn't look promising.

She and Logan were still barely visible at the corner of the building, but the attackers' backs were turned to the street; the responders were too busy fending off the crazies to notice them.

"This is certifiably insane!" The male responder jabbed his gloved finger at Bandanna. "I've had it with you people! Take your circus somewhere else!"

Dakota agreed with him. Every word he'd said was correct, but it wasn't the right move. Instead of defusing the situation, the tension ramped up tenfold.

He was trying to be the hero, but he'd just made things worse.

The tough, muscled Latino in the black tank top who'd been hanging back, mostly watching, shifted and lifted his pistol slightly. His face darkened. "You people? What the hell does that mean?"

"That a racist remark?" Pinstripe growled. "You a bigot? That why you couldn't bother yourself to get down here before now?" His voice rose. "Is that why you let my wife die?"

"What the hell? No!" the male responder sputtered angrily. "I'm volunteering for this, you festering buttholes—"

"Park!" the female responder warned sharply.

"You threatening us now?" Bandanna stalked up to him, halting a couple feet away. He towered over the short first responder, whose head only reached Bandanna's bulky chest.

Still, the guy didn't back down an inch. His gloved hands were balled into trembling fists. He was losing it.

"Enough!" he exploded. "Everybody back the hell up, right now!"

"No, I don't think I will." Bandanna lifted the length of rebar like a sword and pressed it to the guy's throat. "I'll take that radiation suit you've got, right now."

They were crazed, out of their minds from pain, desperation, and shock. Logic and reasoning weren't even making a dent.

They were going to seriously hurt someone.

Instinctively, Dakota started forward.

"What're you doing?" Logan hissed. He grabbed her arm and pulled her back around the corner of the coffee shop.

"Those are first responders!" she whispered fiercely. "They're risking their lives to help people."

He blinked at her. "Still not a good idea."

She lifted the M4 carbine and pressed the butt against her shoulder. "We should help them."

"We're not in danger. If we get involved, it'll waste time, energy, and someone will get hurt. Likely us. Those people are psychos. They could attack for no reason at all."

"Like they're doing now—to innocent people."

Even as she spoke, part of her agreed with him. It was past 5:40 p.m. and they hadn't even reached Palm Cove yet, though they were close now.

They'd already been out here longer than planned. Every minute they spent in the hot zone exposed them to more radiation.

Every minute wasted might be the difference between life and death for Eden.

In a crisis, you only took care of yourself and your own.

That was the first rule of survival.

Ezra hadn't taught her that. That one, she'd learned on her own.

And yet...

Ezra helped you. He took her and Eden in when he could have turned them away or even shot them.

Sister Rosemarie saved you, too. The woman had risked her own safety for Dakota and Eden when she smuggled them the key to the compound gate and helped them escape.

Sometimes, there was nothing you could do for someone, and you just had to push forward and find a way to shed the guilt.

But sometimes, you could do something. This wasn't like the trapped, grievously wounded victims they could do nothing for. They could actually stop this.

All her life, she'd loathed the people who witnessed her suffering and stood by and did nothing. She sure as hell wasn't going to let the apocalypse turn her into one of those assholes.

"We're not animals," she said, as much to herself as to Logan. "And we're not the bad guys."

Logan gave an indifferent shrug. "Speak for yourself. I signed up to help you get your sister and win myself a safehouse, not play vigilante against armed crazies."

She grasped for anything. "What about honor?"

"Honor isn't so much a motivating factor for me. Try something a bit more appealing—like a naked woman, or better yet, a vat full of vodka."

She glared at him. "Your morality?"

He stared back at her, blinking rapidly. His eyes were bloodshot. "Alas. I must have misplaced it."

She restrained herself from punching him in the face. "Fine, be a worthless drunk. I'm not leaving them."

Logan seized her upper arm. The careless, nonchalant mask dropped from his face. His expression was tense, his mouth tight. "Wait—you don't have any bullets."

She shook him off. "They don't know that, do they?"

Dakota turned away from him, rounded the corner, and marched toward the group, her empty carbine lifted and ready.

She was reasonably confident she could control this. She'd scare them with the M4, startle them into backing off—and quickly.

She was outnumbered, but they were wounded, and only one of them had a gun.

That put the odds a little more in her favor, at least.

She didn't know the best play in this situation. She hated winging anything. But there was no time; the ragged mob was closing in on the two first responders.

Blondie and Hawaii were pawing at the woman, trying to rip off her respirator mask, while Bandanna pressed the jagged edge of the rebar against the male responder's suited throat.

These people weren't thinking clearly about anything anymore. They were crazed with grief, pain, and shock. They only wanted blood.

She was out of time.

For an instant, she hesitated. Maybe this was a mistake.

There would be a cost to getting involved. There always was.

Maybe the price for helping these people would be higher than she knew, higher than she could afford to pay.

But she had to do something. How could she live with herself if she just walked away?

Icy adrenaline surged through her veins. She tasted fear on her tongue, sharp and metallic as blood.

One, two, three. Breathe.

Go.

"Hey!" She planted her feet and leveled the muzzle of the carbine at the center of Tank Top's spine. "Stop right now!"

23

LOGAN

Logan watched the waitress march out to face the deranged maniacs like some kamikaze cowboy.

She was as insane as they were.

This wasn't his business. Wasn't his problem. He should just walk away, hightail it out of the hot zone, save himself and find someplace to hunker down...

And then what? Get good and drunk, that's what. Even more than he was now. And stay punch-drunk until the world fixed itself again.

But that wasn't going to happen.

Besides, his world was already fractured. Bombs and anarchy had nothing to do with his own damaged soul.

He'd been spiraling the drain for years. And he knew it.

He glanced back at Shay and Julio, who waited as instructed, huddled behind the burned-out husk of the classic Firebird, Julio fingering his gold cross and murmuring prayers, Shay chewing anxiously on her fingernails.

Shay was a healer; Julio, a kind and gentle soul, was a peacemaker. Neither of them was cut out to be a warrior.

He was, though.

He hadn't lied to Dakota, but he had allowed her to assume what she'd wanted to. She knew the truth now. He was no soldier.

But he *was* a fighter. And a damn good one.

When he wasn't drunk. He felt the alcohol in his blood, buzzing in his veins. Dulling his senses, his thoughts coming slow and sluggish.

He forced himself to roll up his sleeve and look down at the barbed wire tattoo on his forearm, at the elegant cursive letters of the Latin inscription: *et facti sunt ne unum.*

Lest you become one.

He'd inked it one month before that fateful night, five months before the arrest, the sentencing, the barred door slamming shut on his cell.

It was a warning, a last-ditch effort to hold himself back from the abyss.

It had failed.

He knew well his own darkness, no matter how deep down he shoved it. He knew his own tendency to push past the line, to unleash that thing inside him that craved bloodshed at any cost— and enjoyed it.

He stared down at the pistol still in his hands, at his scarred knuckles, the tattoos rippling up his muscled arms.

That was his old life. His street life. His prison life. He'd put it all far behind him.

It was the only way he could live with himself. No matter how far he'd fallen, he still kept that one promise.

She was going to make him break it.

"Damn it, girl," he muttered.

Adrenaline spiked through him, anticipation thrumming through his veins. It wasn't enough to burn off the dullness of the booze still sloshing through him. His senses felt blunted. He cursed himself for those last several beers.

But there was no helping things now.

He was a fighter. He would fight.

He flexed his hands, willing himself to shake off the haze. He tightened his grip on the pistol and stepped back to hide most of his body behind the protective wall of the coffee shop.

Dakota halted about thirty feet from the frenzied hostiles, the carbine aimed at the closest one. "Stop right now!"

Most of them spun to face her.

The Latino guy in the red bandanna didn't. Instead, he jabbed the short male responder in the chest with the pointed end of the length of rebar. The man stumbled.

Before he could recover, Bandanna twisted, cocked his arms back, and swung the rebar at the man's skull.

The man cringed and flung his arm up defensively.

Instead of striking his head, the metal club slammed into his forearm. A terrible, resounding *thwack* echoed in the still air.

The responder gave a wet scream, staggered, and fell against the pole. The back of his head cracked against metal. His body sagged to the asphalt.

The female responder fell to her knees next to him with a strangled cry. "What did you do?"

Bandanna pushed her out of the way. He laughed as he jerked off the man's respirator mask and held it aloft.

The male responder crumpled in on himself, clutching his mangled right arm. The forearm was bent at a strange, unnatural angle, the hand hanging limply.

Just who did these asshats think they were? They were victims themselves—until they'd chosen to prey on someone else.

Indignation sparked through Logan, sank its black claws into his brain.

He couldn't help it. The rage was in him now. The desire to fight, to hurt.

They would pay for it. Logan would make them pay.

24

LOGAN

Instead of following Dakota out into the open, Logan stayed low and skirted the rear of the coffee shop, taking the side alley, avoiding piles of debris and a dumpster turned on its side.

The stench of rotting food mingled with a scorched plastic smell fermented in the heat. Nausea roiled in his gut. He blinked to clear his head.

He crouched behind the dumpster for cover, tension humming through him. Slow and silent, he adjusted his grip on the Glock and slivered back the slide to check the brass in the chamber.

Four out of seven 9mm rounds left.

His stomach sank, sour acid climbing up his throat. He cursed himself for forgetting the three spare magazines tucked in the glove compartment of his '98 Honda Civic—still parked in the Beer Shack's parking lot.

That was the downside to the compact Glock 43: fewer bullets.

Still, he had no desire to shoot anyone. He'd already done that today. Once he showed himself, things would escalate quickly. If there was any way to avoid bloodshed, he would take it.

He stayed hidden and scoped out the scene. He had a clear view between the dumpster and the faux brick wall of the coffee shop.

The blonde chick, Hawaiian shirt guy, and the one in the suit didn't look like experienced fighters or marksmen as far as Logan could tell. Tank knew how to handle the gun. And Bandanna hadn't even hesitated before he'd attacked the male responder. He was no stranger to violence.

Tank and Bandanna were both Latino and heavily tattooed.

Three non-factors, two experienced fighters. Logan should be able to take them if he had to, inebriated or not. Hopefully, Dakota could handle this on her own.

"Leave them alone!" Dakota shouted from ten yards away. "Get lost!"

She stood tall and defiant, her feet shoulder-width apart, her long auburn hair swinging behind her, looking like a crazy badass with that carbine jammed against her shoulder, the business end aimed at the chest of the burly hostile with the gun.

"Just walk away now," she warned them. "Walk away and I won't blast a dozen holes in your sorry asses like you deserve."

The guy in the tank top holding the pistol, Hawaiian shirt with the butcher knife, Bandanna with the rebar spear, and Pinstripe with the double tire irons all turned as one to face her.

Their eyes widened in surprise and fear when they saw the wicked-looking M4. Behind them, Blondie let out a startled gasp. Pinstripe and Hawaii both took a step back, their arms lifting, though they didn't drop their weapons.

Only Tank didn't flinch.

"Hey, now," Pinstripe said uneasily. "There's no need for that. Why don't you put that thing down?"

"We weren't causing no trouble," Blondie said and spat blood out of the corner of her mouth. She moved in front of the male

122

responder, still groaning on the ground, as if Dakota hadn't seen it all.

"Lower your weapons," Dakota said.

Blondie and Pinstripe both started to obey. Hawaii wavered. Bandanna gave Tank a questioning glance. Like they knew each other.

Tank gave a hard shake of his head. He didn't lower his pistol. If anything, he raised it a little, so it was aimed at her legs.

Hawaii followed his cue and kept his own weapon. So did Bandanna. Tank was clearly the man in charge.

"That's a big rifle for such a little girl," Tank growled. He had twitchy eyes and a hard, slippery smile. Logan didn't like the look of him, not at all.

"Big enough to get the job done," Dakota snapped.

"Where'd you even get that?" Hawaii asked. "You steal that off the body of some poor soldier?"

Hawaii acted as tough as Tank, but Logan noted that he took a slow, careful step to the side, out of the path of the M4's muzzle.

Tank, on the other hand, did not. His smile only broadened. "How shameful."

"That rifle look familiar to you?" Bandanna asked Tank with a scowl.

"Sure does." Tank's gaze lowered to the M4. "You didn't take that from one of our boys, did you, little girl?"

Logan stiffened. So they were Blood Outlaws. At least, Tank and Bandanna were. The other three just seemed to be random people who'd fallen in with them after the chaos of the blast.

To her credit, Dakota didn't take the bait. She shifted, tracking the muzzle between Bandanna, Hawaii, and Tank. "Get out of here, all of you."

"Nah, I don't think we will," Tank said.

"You even know how to use that thing?" Hawaii asked.

"I doubt it," Bandanna said with a sly grin.

"I guarantee you don't want to find out," Dakota said.

"You and I both know you don't have a clue how to handle a weapon like that," Tank said. "Why don't you give it to someone who does?"

"Maybe we shouldn't—" Pinstripe started hesitantly, but Tank shot him a vicious look. Pinstripe fell silent.

"You don't have the balls to fire that thing, in more ways than one," Tank said with a hard chuckle.

Hawaii laughed. There was a hint of unease in his voice, but it was fading fast. With every passing second that she didn't pull the trigger, they gained more confidence.

They were underestimating Dakota. In most situations, she could work that to her advantage. But now, when bluffing was her only play, it hurt her big time.

Logan cursed under his breath. If it were him brandishing the assault rifle—a tall, imposing Colombian covered in tattoos—things would be playing out very differently.

Dakota refused to be cowed. She took another step toward them. "I said back off!"

Tank only sneered. "Why don't you let a real man handle that for you? We're happy to take that beauty off your hands."

Bandanna followed his lead. Emboldened by Tank's scornful dismissiveness toward the potential threat, he took a step toward Dakota and brandished his rebar, slapping the metal against the palm of his hand as if challenging her to come at him.

"Stop right there or I shoot!" Dakota ordered.

Tank flashed a dangerous smile. "We just want the gun. We'll let you go." He paused. "I promise."

"Speak for yourself," Hawaii said, scowling. "What else you got hiding around here? You're too clean and untouched. You been hiding out somewhere watching the rest of us suffer?"

"No—"

"You keeping it all to yourself, is that it?" He licked his cracked lips. "You got untainted food? Medical supplies? A working cellphone?"

"No!"

"No," Bandanna said as he took another step toward her, his features contorting in pain and rage. "She says no. I say we find out for ourselves. And we'll start with that gun."

Logan took a steadying breath and refocused his aim. These scumbags were beyond reason. They were desperate to enact vengeance for their suffering, for what they'd lost.

And if they couldn't find the people to blame, they'd scapegoat someone else.

Blondie remained beneath the sagging gas station roof beside their victims, guarding them. But the others spread out across the glass-littered parking lot, Pinstripe hobbling toward Dakota from the left, Hawaii stalking her from the right, Bandanna facing her straight on while Tank circled to get behind her.

Dakota swung the carbine back and forth, trying to keep the nearest threat in her sights, but there were too many of them. "I said don't move!"

"Like I said, you're not gonna shoot that thing," Tank said from three yards behind her, his pistol—a Sig Sauer 226—aimed at her head.

"Try me." Dakota started to whirl to face him, correctly surmising he was the greatest threat, even though Bandanna had attacked the responders first. They were both dangerous.

Tank fired a warning shot over her head. The crack echoed impossibly loud.

Dakota froze, still facing away from Tank.

"Next one will tunnel right through your skull, understand?"

Dakota lifted her chin. "Go ahead, but I'll take out a few of you first."

"Doubt it," Tank said dismissively. "Now lower the gun, nice and slow, and give it to me."

"And if I don't?"

Tank fingered the trigger. "Haven't I already warned you once?"

This situation was going downhill fast.

Logan gritted his teeth so hard his head hurt. Two days ago, these were just regular people like everyone else, survivors of a horror none of them could comprehend.

But they'd let their fear overtake them and twist them into something else—something grotesque and monstrous. They were unleashing their terror on the very people who'd risked so much to help them.

Or maybe they had always been monsters, kept caged by society until the bombing. Now they were unleashed, free to prey on others.

He'd bet everything he owned that Tank and Bandanna were natural-born predators. Maybe Blood Outlaws, maybe not. It didn't matter.

Their eyes were bright, their mouths twisted into hard smiles. He recognized that look on their faces. They were enjoying this. They took pleasure in inciting fear and pain in others.

Logan knew how to be a predator, too.

He inched out from behind the dumpster, readying himself. He rose onto one knee, rested his forearms on his thigh to steady his hands, and aimed through his sights at Tank's skull.

The gun wavered slightly. His vision blurred. Sour acid stung the back of his throat. He blinked fiercely, forcing himself to focus.

Pinstripe was blocking his view.

If he took Pinstripe out first, he'd lose a precious second, enough time for Tank to pull the trigger and kill Dakota.

The alcohol had slowed his reaction time. He knew that with

dead certainty. But the question was, how much? Did he dare risk it?

Pinstripe slowly lowered his tire irons. "I don't know. She's just a girl. Maybe this is too much. Let's just go, man."

"She was trying to kill you," Bandanna snarled. "She'd kill all of us. After we survived the bomb? Hell, no."

"Let those people go," Dakota said, her voice firm and steady. "Then you can all walk away."

She looked tense but not terrified. She wasn't panicking. That was good.

"Leave us alone!" The female responder hunched over her fallen partner, cradling his head on her lap. "Just stop!"

The wounded male responder only moaned.

"They didn't do this to you," Dakota said to Pinstripe, the only one who seemed capable of backing down. "They were trying to help you, not hurt you."

Pinstripe only shook his head, reluctant but unwilling to stop the others. He was still just as culpable in Logan's book.

"Shut the hell up!" Bandanna said.

"Everyone out there, they've abandoned us to our fate," Tank said bitterly. "No one cares what happens to us. Why should we care what happens to you?"

Tank strode closer to Dakota. Finally, Logan's view was clear, but now Tank's muzzle was inches from the back of Dakota's skull.

Logan couldn't risk the shot.

"Don't think I need to tell you again, do I?" Tank said. "Drop it like a good little girl."

Slowly, Dakota lifted the strap of the M4 over her head and lowered the carbine to the pavement. The muzzle of Tank's Sig moved with her.

"Go to hell," Dakota spat.

"I think you know we're already there." Tank gave a twisted

smile. "And if we're in hell anyway, who says we can't have a bit of fun while we're here?"

Tank struck Dakota on the side of the head with the butt of the gun.

Dakota let out a harsh, startled breath. She fell hard to her hands and knees.

Tank smiled as he lifted the gun, his finger on the trigger.

2 5

LOGAN

A ferocious anger slammed through Logan.

He didn't believe in much, cared about even less.

The waitress was stubborn, arrogant, infuriating. But she had balls of steel. And she was a hell of a lot braver than he was.

Seeing her like that—down on the ground, hurt, humiliated, and vulnerable—it flipped a switch inside him.

Something dark and brutal and remorseless clawed its way out.

He wanted to hurt and be hurt, to do damage with his hands, his fists, his whole body.

The world sharpened and blurred and sharpened again. Sound faded away but for the rush of blood in his ears. He tensed, teeth clenched, lips bared.

He let the outrage flow over him, into him, through him.

Then he moved.

One second, he was hanging back, still taking in the lay of the land, watching Dakota receive the brunt of the hostiles' aggression.

In the next instant, he was up and charging, already among them before they were even aware of his presence, a hurricane of savage fury.

He fired a round into Pinstripe's non-wounded leg as he ran past. It wasn't a kill shot, but the man screamed with a high, animal sound, his arms windmilling backward, the tire irons slipping from his limp fingers.

He collapsed, his ruined leg twitching convulsively.

One down.

Logan aimed and fired at Tank's forehead as he ran. It was a difficult shot to nail on the move, especially with his senses dulled, his reactions blunted.

A shot he would've made if his head was clear.

He knew even as he pulled the trigger that the round would miss its target, but Logan needed to make himself the greater threat immediately.

As he expected, the shot went wide, whistling past the left side of Tank's neck and drilling into the stucco façade of an apartment building thirty feet behind him.

Tank whirled, surprised but already raising his Sig as he swiveled his thick, muscular body to face Logan.

Instinctively, Logan ducked and pulled back as the muzzle arced toward him.

The loud crack exploded in his ears. A zinging sting slashed across the top of his right ear.

The bullet missed his skull by a hair's breadth.

He stayed low and rushed toward Tank, who came at him with a sadistic growl. They collided in a crash of heavy bodies, grappling for each other's guns, each trying to jam their weapons into soft, viable flesh.

Tank managed to elbow Logan hard in the face, jabbing at him with the pistol's muzzle, attempting to aim and shoot, but Logan was too fast.

The man missed again.

The blast of the shot was so close it made his ears ring.

Logan pummeled the man with a flurry of vicious blows, but Tank hammered right back.

Pain exploded in Logan's ribs, his shoulder. He feinted high and dodged in low. He was a fraction of a second slower than he needed to be.

Still, the blow landed.

He slammed his fist in a brutal uppercut, the punch catching Tank beneath the chin, snapping his head back and toppling him over in one swift movement.

The Sig flew from his hands, pinwheeled in the air, and skittered across the pavement.

Logan stepped close and aimed for Tank's right shoulder to permanently disable him. His vision went blurry. He blinked, wavering slightly.

Tank rolled onto his back, grabbed a handful of powdered rubble, and hurled it at Logan's face. Logan reared back, coughing, clawing at his stinging eyes with his free hand.

Tank nailed Logan's gun with a well-aimed kick, striking his hand and knocking it free. Logan reached for it blindly, but it spun away.

Tank lunged for his legs to knock him off his feet. Logan dodged out of the way, turned, and delivered a sharp kick to the man's face.

The back of his skull punched the pavement, stunning him. He groaned and stayed down, at least for the moment.

Logan wiped his face furiously. He blinked hard, searching through stinging, half-lidded eyes for the tiny Glock 43 in the debris-littered parking lot.

Tank was stronger and faster than he'd expected. He needed his gun. He needed to end this, fast.

From the corner of his squinting eye, he saw a vague, bleary figure barreling toward him from the left. He glimpsed a slash of red.

Bandanna, rushing at him full-tilt.

The world swayed and blurred around him. His reaction time was too slow, too dulled. There was no time for a counter move, only a desperate, half-assed block.

Logan half-twisted, raising his arm defensively.

Bandanna lifted the deadly length of rebar, stabbing like a sword.

26

LOGAN

Logan flinched, anticipating the pain of the blow.

Out of nowhere, Dakota charged at Bandanna with the carbine in both hands, gripping it by the handguard. An instant before the hostile reached Logan, she cracked the stock across the back of the man's skull.

Bandanna staggered and fell, knocking against Logan's left leg and nearly sweeping him off his feet.

Logan flung out his arms, swaying, his stomach lurching.

He managed to regain his balance and stepped sideways, stomping as hard as he could against the fuzzy shape of Bandanna's outstretched hand as he reached for the fallen rebar.

Flesh and bone crunched beneath his boot.

The man let out an inhuman wail and curled in on himself, clutching his crushed hand to his chest.

Through bleary eyes, Logan focused on the dark circle of Bandanna's face. He shattered the man's nose—and rendered him unconscious—with a solid kick.

He took half a second to wipe the grit from his eyes and blink away the stinging tears.

For an instant, he and Dakota made eye contact.

Someone had gotten a good punch in. Her lip was cut. Scarlet droplets stained her shirt.

"You okay?" he asked, already half-turning to take in the rest of the scene, searching for Tank. The man wouldn't stay down for long.

She grinned ferociously at him, her teeth bloody.

A flash of movement from behind her.

"Watch out!" he shouted.

Blondie had abandoned her guard duties to join the fight. She screamed and rushed at Dakota, tire iron clenched in both hands.

Dakota whipped around, using the carbine as a club. She swung at the woman's torso and nailed her in the gut. Blondie went down, writhing, clutching her stomach and sucking in air.

Behind her, Logan glimpsed the female responder dragging her partner back into the shadows beneath the sagging roof of the gas station, getting them both clear of the fight.

Blondie leapt to her feet, scrambling for Dakota. Dakota stepped back and raised the carbine defensively, warding off several blows.

Logan moved to come to her aid.

With a shriek of fury, Hawaii rushed him from the right, swinging with the butcher knife.

In two quick paces, Logan sidestepped and then leapt, striking Hawaii sideways. They fell together, the knife scraping his ribs. Logan barely felt it.

Instantly up again, he whirled and kicked the fallen man on the chin as he struggled to rise. Hawaii's teeth clacked, and blood spurted from his mouth and nose.

The knife slid from his fingers.

Blondie howled like a banshee and hurled herself at Dakota. She struck with the tire iron, swinging low and lifting it like a baseball bat, hitting the carbine from beneath, snagging the hanging strap and nearly breaking Dakota's fingers.

To save her hands, Dakota dropped the carbine and flung herself backward.

She scrambled to her feet and came up swinging with her tactical knife.

Dakota could take care of herself. Logan needed to focus on his own battles. He returned his attention to Hawaii.

The fat man had climbed to his knees, searching the debris for his knife.

Logan scooped up one of the tire irons Pinstripe had dropped, took two fast steps, and swung it at the man as hard as he could.

It struck his freshly wounded face with a wet thud. Bone and cartilage cracked and shattered.

Hawaii let out a stunned, agonized cry. He collapsed and stayed down.

The hostile was no longer a threat. Logan could stop now, but he didn't want to. He couldn't.

A distant roar filled his ears, savage, relentless, urging him on. He smelled his own rage like the scent of burning rubber, something dark and pungent and dangerous.

He slammed the tire iron against the side of the man's skull one more time. The solid, satisfying smack reverberated all the way up his arms as he felt the bone give way beneath his fury.

He straightened, wiping sweat and blood from his eyes, searching the parking lot for the next threat, the next hostile to unleash his wrath upon.

Three—no—four bodies down.

Dakota gripped her knife and stood over Blondie, who cowered on the ground, curled into a fetal position and covering her bloodied face with her hands.

She had things under control.

He blinked to clear his vision. His ears were still ringing, his thoughts coming too slow, too jumbled.

He was missing something. Something important.

He turned slowly, his ribs burning, his breath coming in ragged gasps.

Where were the pistols? The Glock and Sig were somewhere nearby, skittered behind a gas pump or hidden in the rubble.

He needed to find them. He needed—

The fifth hostile. Tank.

Where was he?

Logan's blows had been enough to stun him, but not—

"Behind you!" Dakota screamed.

27

LOGAN

Logan had just enough time to whip around and get his forearm up to block the tire iron as Tank plowed into him. He deflected the weapon, the man's arm striking him with only a glancing blow.

They rolled to the ground. Logan caught the wrist of the hand gripping the tire iron and slammed it against the asphalt hard once, twice, three times.

Tank let out a pained shriek. His fingers released their grip. The tire iron clattered away.

Logan attempted to push up to get to his feet, but Tank reached back to claw at the back of his head, trying to flip him.

Logan squirmed, evading him. Gravel, glass shards, and debris scraped painfully against his back.

Tank jerked his head back in a reverse headbutt. Logan sensed the movement and lunged to the side, but reacted a split second too slow.

The back of the man's skull smashed into Logan's cheekbone. Hot pain exploded in his face, stars flashing behind his eyes. His nose spurted blood.

This guy knew how to fight. Despite regular boxing training at the gym, Logan was slow and rusty. Exhaustion and alcohol turned his limbs to lead. His stomach sloshed with nausea. He needed to end this before the thug got the drop on him.

It was only a matter of time.

He sucked in lungfuls of oxygen, readying himself. Gathering every ounce of his dwindling strength, Logan twisted and leapt to his feet, seizing the man as he pivoted.

Leveraging his momentum, he lifted Tank with a strained grunt and slung him as hard as he could into the nearest gas station pole.

Tank bounced off the pole. He half-fell, staggering—but not down, not unconscious. His skull hadn't hit the pole hard enough.

He shook himself off like a dog and pulled himself back to his feet. He bared his teeth in a growl.

Remaining in a low crouch, Logan scanned the parking lot, searching frantically for one of the guns. Too much debris scattered everywhere. He didn't have even a second to spare to hunt for it.

"The gun!" he yelled to Dakota.

Tank spun fast and low and lunged for Logan with another growl, a tactical knife suddenly clenched in his right fist.

Logan barely had time to react to this new information. He threw himself backward, twisting away from the attack, Tank still coming at him with the knife, making short, efficient thrusts with the blade.

Logan scrambled back, almost tripping on a large slab of drywall in a landslide of rubble, his vision wavering, everything tilting sideways.

He regained his balance and darted around a gas pump, putting it between him and the hostile.

Undaunted, Tank kept rushing him, relentless, stabbing and slashing with that knife. He faltered for a second, slipping on a roof shingle, but it barely slowed him down.

This wasn't working. He was tired and slow. He had seconds before Tank reached him. A few slashes with that blade and it would all be over.

Logan needed to try something else.

He faked a stumble, nearly falling. As he did, he shifted his weight to his left foot, allowing him to set up for a roundhouse kick with the right.

Tank bought the ruse.

With a victorious gleam in his eyes, he darted in close, swiping the knife at Logan's face, trying to blind him.

Logan raised his forearm, blocking the blows, and threw the kick. His shin connected with the side of the hostile's kneecap, buckling it with a nasty crack.

Groaning in pain and surprise, Tank collapsed to his knees.

Logan grabbed the man's head and jabbed his right thumb deep into his right eye socket. The soft globe rolled beneath his digging fingernail.

Something popped wetly.

Tank howled in agony.

With his left hand, Logan seized the man's right wrist, holding the knife safely away. With his right fist, he battered the guy's head and face, punching him again and again, smashing and hammering in blind, brutal fury.

Blood spurted from Tank's nose and mouth, smearing Logan's hands. Pain seared his split knuckles, his bruised ribs, his chest. He barely felt it through the pumping adrenaline, over his bucking, plunging heart.

He thought only of beating this pathetic pissant into a bloody pulp, and then beating him some more.

Abruptly, Tank crumpled onto his back, yanking Logan down with him.

Logan's grip on the man's wrist slipped in the slick, treacherous blood.

In one swift move, Tank twisted and flipped.

Logan's brain registered the action, but the synapses firing to his muscles were a fraction too slow.

He couldn't react in time.

Tank leapt on top of Logan, slamming the back of his head against the concrete, forearm punched against his throat.

Stars burst behind Logan's eyes, his vision exploding with red and black. He tried to whip the guy off, but his limbs were suddenly sluggish. They wouldn't obey him.

He couldn't get his hands up swiftly enough, couldn't defend against the attack he knew was coming.

Tank was simply too fast.

The man's eyes were hard little slits in his bruised and bloody face. He didn't bother to gloat; he went straight for the kill shot.

He raised his knife and slashed toward Logan's chest.

2 8

LOGAN

Boom!

A small hole appeared in the side of Tank's head.

The knife slipped from the man's lax hand.

He went slack, his mouth frozen in a startled O. His heavy body collapsed on top of Logan, limp and unmoving.

Logan's ears rang. He couldn't breathe. Blood dripped onto his cheek and slid down his jaw. His ribs burned like they'd been raked with coals.

He didn't care. He didn't care about any of it.

His heart was still beating—he heard it like a roaring rush in his ears.

He was alive.

He was alive, and Tank was dead.

Logan heaved two hundred and fifty pounds of dead weight to the asphalt and pulled himself to his feet, brushing dust and debris from his clothes.

He wrenched his neck as he turned quickly, scanning the area for potential threats. But there weren't any left.

The fight was over.

Tank was dead. Pinstripe was still on the ground, groaning, clutching his leg. Blood leaked from both bullet holes, but Logan's rounds hadn't hit an artery. He would live if he got medical attention soon enough.

Blondie slumped next to him. Her face was covered in blood. She raised her hands in surrender.

Bandanna sagged against the nearest gas pump, his crushed hand nestled against his chest, out cold. Several feet to the left, Hawaii's body lay at an awkward angle, a spreading puddle leaking onto the asphalt beneath his head.

Dakota stood less than eight feet away, her legs shoulder-width apart, both hands gripping Tank's 9mm Sig Sauer, the muzzle still pointed exactly where she'd aimed.

Logan sucked in a sharp breath. "That was a damn hard shot."

Her face was leached of color, her eyes so wide he could see the whites all the way around. "I know."

"You could've killed me."

She lowered the gun but kept it in the ready position. "But I didn't."

Most people got panicky and shaky in real life-and-death situations. The waitress could've easily shot him instead.

He shook his head, marveling at how close he'd come to getting his own face blown off. "Holy hell."

"I guess practicing three times a week at the range finally paid off." She gave a little shrug. "In all honesty, I wasn't sure I could pull it off. But even if I missed and hit you, I figured you were dead anyway. I had to take the shot."

"I'm glad you did."

Dakota turned and gestured at Blondie with the Sig. "I've got plenty of bullets left. I'd rather not waste them on you. Get out of here."

Without a word, Blondie helped Pinstripe to his feet. They stumbled down a side street in the opposite direction, a trail of blood splattering the road behind them.

Logan spat sour spittle out of the corner of his mouth and wiped away the blood trickling from his nose. His eyes still stung from the handful of dust and dirt Tank had thrown at him. He blinked hard and rubbed his face.

The rage and adrenaline drained out of him, leaving behind a hollow emptiness.

The pain rushed in then. Nausea swept his guts. Acid surged up his throat. He bent over, spitting watery vomit. He dry-heaved several times before his stomach settled enough to straighten.

His body always responded this way after a particularly vicious fight—especially one with a dead body or two.

He never felt it during. Afterward, he felt everything.

"Logan."

He blinked again, swaying slightly. Everything felt distant and far away, disconnected, his body still heavy and sluggish.

"Logan!"

He looked at Dakota. She was wiping blood from her split lip with the back of her arm. She held the Sig limply at her side. She was bruised, but alive.

"You okay?" he managed.

"Hell of a headache. I've got a bump literally the size of an egg." She grimaced and spat more blood. "But I'll live. I should ask you that question."

He went through the motions of checking himself for injuries, running his hands over his body. His ribs on his left side hurt like hell. He raised his shirt. A nasty slash about five inches long raked his side.

It wasn't deep, but it hurt like a mother.

Small cuts stung his hands and knuckles. The top of his right ear was missing a chunk of cartilage from the round that had nearly ended him. He'd also earned a split lip and probably a black eye along with several bruises, but no permanent damage.

"I'm fine," he lied. He wasn't fine. It felt like he'd never be fine again. "It just...takes me a minute...after."

"Yeah, I know what you mean." Dakota stooped and unstrapped the holster from Tank's dead body and fixed it to her own belt, then tucked the Sig inside. She pulled the Glock from her waistband and handed it to him. "I found this one, too."

He checked it quickly and then holstered it. "Thanks."

He started to rub his face again.

"Logan!" Dakota said sharply. "Don't touch anything with your hands. You were rolling around in all that contaminated dust. You should wash out your eyes. And we need to get Shay to wipe you down."

"Yeah...sorry." He let his hands fall limply at his sides. You'd think you wouldn't forget about the radiation for a hot second, but it was more difficult than he'd thought.

Habits died hard. Twenty-five years of doing things one way versus six hours out in this hostile, brutal hellhole.

They should go find Shay and Julio. And check on the first responders, wherever they'd crawled off to in order to escape the fighting. He needed to wash the filth off himself. They needed to get moving, get the heck out of the hot zone.

But he didn't move. His legs were like lead. Nausea roiled through him. He still felt weak, like if he took a step, he might collapse.

And if he were completely truthful with himself, he wasn't ready to see anyone else yet, to be peppered with questions he had no desire to answer.

None of them knew what it was like to fight for your life, to grapple with another human being, to beat someone bloody with your bare fists.

Just one minute. One damn minute and then he'd force himself to return to the chaos. He sucked in a sharp breath. Maybe two minutes.

Dakota's brow wrinkled. "You saved my ass."

"I think it's safe to say that you saved mine in return."

That earned a tight smile. "Yeah, I did."

"You're not bad with a gun," he forced out, pretending at cool composure. "Who taught you to shoot?"

"My crazy prepper friend. Who taught you to fight?"

"I picked up a few tips here and there." He gave a nonchalant shrug, turning slightly so she wouldn't see the pained grimace he couldn't hide.

He rubbed his sore, bloody knuckles, scarred from dozens of street fights. His hands were already dirty, what did it matter? Blood speckled the five-dot tattoo between his thumb and pointer finger. He wiped it on his pants.

It was Alejandro Gomez, second in command of the MS-13 chapter in Richmond, Virginia, who had taken him in like his own son, gave him a roof over his head, a job, a brotherhood.

After a lonely childhood devoid of anything resembling love, at sixteen Logan had thirsted for any affection he could beg, buy, or steal. Alejandro had seen something in the nervy street kid who threw himself full-tilt into any and every fight, never backing down, never flinching, never shying from a split lip or black eye.

Alejandro had offered him what no one else had before —belonging.

And then he had taught Logan, mentored him, trained him to be his righthand man, his muscle, his killing arm.

His assassin.

He had done everything his mentor had asked of him. And then he'd done more.

Until the day he couldn't anymore, and prison and death became better options than the monster he'd become.

After prison, he'd fled the state and never looked back.

His demons had followed him anyway.

29

LOGAN

Logan watched Dakota as she reached up as if to retie her sagging ponytail, remembered not to touch herself, and dropped her arms.

She saw him looking and stared back at him, defiant. But her face was still pale, her pupils huge. Her hands were trembling.

This wasn't like the woman with the dead baby, whose life she ended out of pity. She'd killed a man in cold blood. She'd killed him for Logan.

Another wave of nausea struck him. He bent, hands on his thighs, letting the blood rush to his head. His ears were still ringing. He tasted the coppery tang of blood in his mouth, between his teeth.

Everything inside him felt sharp and jagged as broken glass.

"Killing isn't like the movies," he said haltingly. "Unless you're a psychopath, taking a life always has a cost."

"I know that."

She said it like she really did, like she had experience with killing. Once again, he found himself surprised by this girl.

"There's always a consequence," she said. "But if it protects someone I care about, then I'll gladly pay that price."

He looked at her. Really looked at her. The waning sunlight highlighted the strands of red in her hair, the sharp planes of her face, the glisten of her wide dark eyes.

He'd noticed her the past few months working the tables at the Beer Shack—but only like he noticed everyone, sizing them up for potential threats then letting them go in his mind.

She was just another young, dark-haired girl in a city of millions.

But now he saw things he hadn't before. Her long, messy auburn hair spilling past her shoulders, several damp strands curling against her cheeks. The dust caking her thick eyebrows, her solid jaw jutting proudly, those hard, flinty eyes cutting straight through him.

She was beautiful the way a piece of cut glass was beautiful— and just as sharp.

Dakota narrowed her eyes. "Glad you finally grew a conscience back there."

"I wouldn't go that far." Logan dropped his gaze and kicked at a pile of rubble with his boot. He hesitated, working his jaw before asking the question. "Don't you feel guilty?"

"For this scumbag? No." She raised her chin as if daring him to contradict her. "Not even a little."

He was never sure which was worse: living with the guilt or not feeling it at all.

He'd never doubted his decisions, his choices, even deriving a vicious pleasure at justice served, at taking vengeance into his own hands.

He'd felt no guilt or remorse for any of the men he'd hurt or killed, criminals and thieves and murderers, all of them—not until the mother and the kid.

He hadn't wanted to care. He'd tried to convince himself it was an accident, a mistake, tried to put it from his mind the way he'd done a dozen times before.

It hadn't worked.

He still saw the tiny figure that haunted his nightmares—the saggy Spiderman pajama bottoms, the thin arms clutching a ratty stuffed bear. And that small face framed by black curly hair disheveled from sleep, those wide dark eyes staring back at him, so young, so trusting.

He knew what he'd done. He knew the truth. And the truth ate at him, hounding him, consuming him from the inside out.

"You shouldn't feel guilty, either." Dakota's eyes softened. "Not for this."

He went still. "For what?"

She pointed behind him. "For that."

He turned slowly, his split knuckles flexing and unflexing, apprehension curdling his stomach.

He'd forgotten about Hawaii, about what he'd done to him in his adrenaline-fueled rage.

With growing dread, Logan nudged Hawaii's body with his foot.

Bone shards protruded from the back of the man's skull. Something slick and pulpy oozed out. Brain tissue.

The man was dead.

That familiar, sick-spinning horror twisted inside him. Despair clawed at his throat. Despair—and thirst.

He needed a drink. He was desperate for it. He needed to drown every shadowy demon until he felt nothing but numbness.

He'd done this. He'd killed a man.

He'd worked hard to put that part of himself behind a wall and brick it up tight. It was out now, for better or worse.

The darkness, the hunger. The monster.

It's who you are.

Darkness tugged at the edges of his mind, ruthless and unrelenting, threatening to drag him down into its depths. He was at the bottom of a black hole; he couldn't claw his way out.

Not this time.

It's who you've always been.

A merciless, remorseless, stone-cold killer.

You can't escape who you are.

His head ached. His throat burned. That insistent *wanting* seared through him, throbbing through his veins with a dark, pulsing, vicious need.

He needed a drink.

He forced himself to turn away from Hawaii.

He had to get it together. The hot zone was no place to have a nervous breakdown.

He pulled out his flask. He stared down at it, rubbing the gleeful, grinning skull embossed on the front.

He needed to blot out the despair sucking at him. He needed the numbness, the forgetting, needed it like he'd never needed anything in his life.

The demons were out now—hunting him, haunting him.

That small, round face appeared in his mind's eye, those dark, accusing eyes drilling straight through his soul, tormenting him. He could still hear the pleading voice whispering in his head: *You don't need to do this...please...we won't tell...please don't hurt him...*

"Logan?" Dakota was studying him, a faint line between her brows. "Are you sure you're okay?"

He couldn't do it without the booze.

He uncapped the lid and held the flask to his lips. He breathed in the sharp fumes, already tasting them at the back of his tongue. He relished the anticipation of the liquid sliding down his throat.

He'd been slow and sluggish when it counted. He'd almost died today. Would have died, if not for Dakota.

He realized suddenly that he didn't want to die—that was the astonishing thing.

Even more, he didn't want his weakness, his failure to cause harm to Dakota, to Julio or Shay. He'd let his desire to anesthetize himself put everyone at risk.

He'd told himself he didn't care about anything or anyone. That he couldn't. Maybe that was a lie.

He could no longer afford to be numb, to dull his senses, to live in a half-stupor. Not now. Not in this world where the old rules no longer applied.

He was done with drinking. He had to be.

Even if that meant living with the whispers, the demons, the monsters.

Even if that meant they destroyed him.

He didn't look at Dakota. He couldn't bear it. Not now, not in this moment.

His hand shook as he tipped the flask and poured the whiskey out onto the dusty asphalt.

"Logan," Dakota said softly.

He curled his scarred, stained fingers into a fist. Words clotted in his throat. What could he possibly say? "I don't...I'm—"

A groan from behind them drew his attention.

The first responders.

30

MADDOX

Maddox paused beside a body.

Mutilated and wrecked almost beyond recognition, the clothing was in tatters, parts of the body so burned—muscle, tissue, flesh—only charcoaled bones remained.

He couldn't drag his gaze from the face—the eyes melted into a viscous goo, only a few blond wisps of hair remaining on the scalp. And the fleshless grin, all the more grotesque because the lips were entirely gone from the wide grinning mouth, completely burned away...

A fly crawled over the face and disappeared inside the right ear.

More flies followed.

Revulsion burned the back of his throat. What had this person done to deserve such suffering? Whatever the sin, he had no doubt the person had earned it.

He did not feel an ounce of pity for this mangled ruin.

This man and all the others were dead. They'd been punished for their wickedness. He no longer felt pity for anyone, not even himself.

Once, he had been capable of it. Once, he'd pitied a girl. Loved her, even.

But he'd been shown the error of his ways. He had the scars to prove it, did he not?

By the grace of God, he'd been given another chance. A mercy.

Love was a weakness. He'd been weak when he allowed her to escape the first time. But that weakness had been beaten out of him.

Now he was purified, filled only with righteous anger and an urgent, burning sense of purpose.

His father was right. Like all emotions, love was a tool to be manipulated. He had allowed himself to be used, allowed the girl to manipulate and deceive him.

But no longer.

He'd learned from his mistakes.

And now, once again, he had been spared.

Chosen for a purpose.

He clambered over smoking debris, careful not to touch anything. The smoke seared his throat and scorched his lungs. His eyes stung so badly tears streamed down his cheeks.

For two days, he had walked and rested and walked again, journeying through the desolate ruins of the city.

Everything was smoldering. Smoke filled the sky. Up the street, a bank burned furiously. The whole city seemed to be on fire.

For the Lord shall execute judgment by fire...

The heat burned relentlessly through the smoky haze, the south Florida temperature soaring unbearably. His body burned with its own inner heat, his skin hot and clammy.

A part of him wanted to give up, to join the legions of the lost.

But this was a test. A test of his devotion, his endurance, his conviction.

Why else would his father leave him out here in this hell? Why else would the Prophet send him here when he knew the reign of fire was about to descend?

It was a test, and he would pass it.

Just like the sickness clenching his guts was a test.

"Do you need water?" a woman asked him.

He blinked and looked around, startled.

Two women stood not five feet from him on the sidewalk. The first one held out a bottle of water. She wore two backpacks, one on each shoulder, both stuffed full of bottles of water.

A woman next to her had somehow procured a wheelbarrow and filled it with jugs and bottles of water, Gatorade, and apple juice.

He accepted the water and gulped half of it immediately. Sweet and cool, it slid down his parched throat. His empty stomach roiled with nausea.

Without warning, he bent and retched violently. Liquid and sour acid splattered against the asphalt, a few droplets landing on his shoes. Spasms racked his body.

He straightened, wincing, and wiped the back of his mouth.

"You have radiation sickness," the woman said kindly. "There's an emergency field hospital set up not too far from here at Miami Jordan High School. I can give you directions."

He managed a polite smile. "I know where to go, but thank you. You should leave, too." The gift of the water made him feel suddenly charitable, even if he had just vomited it back up. "It's not safe. Any of the buildings could collapse at any moment. Fires are everywhere."

"We're doing God's work," the woman said. A boiling red blister the size of his fist marred the right side of her face. He could see the pink of her scalp where her stubby gray hair had burned away.

"We won't just leave these people to suffer alone," the second woman said loudly, a plump Haitian lady in her fifties.

Lacerations laddered her arms, a dozen cuts marking her broad cheeks and forehead. Dried blood streaked both her ears and trailed down her neck. "We'll do what we can, as long as we can, God willing."

He saw more people now. Ahead of him, a few dozen survivors dug through the rubble of a mid-rise apartment building with sticks of twisted rebar, a few with shovels, others with rag-wrapped or gloved hands.

Their faces were dirty, blackened with soot or smeared with dust, their hair matted against their heads. Every one of them soaked in sweat, many in blood.

"What are they doing?" he asked, perplexed.

"They're getting people out," the hairless woman said proudly. "They're choosing to save lives."

He stuck the bottle of water in his back pocket and watched in astonishment.

In the midst of suffering and misery, people were helping each other.

In addition to the diggers, another handful of people whose wounds weren't debilitating had banded together to pull doors, sheets of corrugated metal, and long planks of wood from the rubble to use as stretchers.

Grimly, they lifted several of the wounded onto their makeshift stretchers and began the slow, painstaking journey through the unstable rubble, ruptured gas lines, sparking tangles of power lines, and fires to safety and medical aid—wherever that may be.

He did not help.

He did not want to help.

Didn't they know they were beyond redemption?

Their actions mattered little now.

It was too late for them. For all of them.

Just like it was too late for Dakota Sloane.

"'Who can endure the heat of his anger? His wrath is poured out like fire, and the rocks are broken into pieces by him,'" he murmured one of the verses his father had forced him to memorize as a child.

"Can you say that again?" asked the woman with all the cuts. With her free hand, she pointed at her bloody ears. "I can't seem to hear too well. I think my eardrums ruptured in the blast."

He just stared at her.

"I'll be fine," she said to the question he hadn't asked. "Thank the Lord I survived. Don't worry about me. I'm blessed, is what I am. Jesus would be out here helping the suffering. We show love through our actions, don't we? It's the least I can do."

Love had nothing to do with it, Maddox thought darkly.

It was as the Prophet had preached all those years, warning them, preparing them. But no one had listened, no one but the faithful few at the compound.

The world was an obscenity. Marred and impure. Contaminated. It could only be purified through fire.

And after the fire, the radiation, descending like an invisible army of vengeance.

Those who believed they'd escaped God's wrath would soon learn the truth, including these forlorn souls digging in the rubble in vain.

Even these two sincere but mistaken women.

He realized suddenly he didn't know how long he'd been walking, the last time he'd stopped to rest. Or even how close he was to his goal.

His stomach wrenched painfully. His body ran boiling hot, then cold, then hot again, sickly sweat stippling his skin.

His head was pulsing now like someone was chipping at his skull with a chisel.

He ignored it all.

He had faith the pain would end soon.

This was a test he would pass.

Maddox smiled benignly down at her. "How far is it to the Palm Cove subdivision? I'm looking for my family. They live on Bellview Court."

"Palm Cove?" said the other woman. She pointed ahead. "Less than a half mile northwest of here."

"God bless you," he said.

31

DAKOTA

"What can we do?" Dakota crouched beside the female responder, who was kneeling deep beneath the shade of the sagging gas station overhang next to the wounded man. Logan stood behind them, standing guard, his pistol in his hands.

The pump next to her was filmed in white dust, the nozzle hose drooping off its hook, dark liquid drizzling from its tip. The air stank of gasoline and smoke.

The smoke stench was stronger now. The fires were getting closer.

The male responder—a short, slight Korean-American man in his thirties—lay on the oil-stained concrete between them, his legs sticking out straight in front of him and elevated by a medical bag.

He had a round, youthful face, his full cheeks slightly pock-marked from old acne scars, the fuzz of a faint mustache above his upper lip. His eyes were closed, but he was conscious, grimacing and hissing labored breaths through gritted teeth.

The rebar blow had missed his skull but struck his right forearm instead. He cradled the arm to his chest. Dakota couldn't see the damage through his bulky PPE suit.

"I need to cut his suit off to get a look at that arm," the woman said briskly.

Dakota unsheathed her knife and handed it to her. She watched as the woman cut through the suit material and freed the man's right arm from his shoulder to his wrist.

His arm looked deformed. A sharp sliver of bone protruded from the skin halfway up his forearm. Blood dripped to the dusty concrete, the droplets bright red against the muted, ashy gray.

"Holy crap," Harlow muttered.

The man groaned. "How—bad is it really?"

"Don't look, Park," Harlow said. "Trust me, you don't want to know."

"Son of a motherless goat," Park mumbled. "It hurts."

"Just don't pass out on me. You may be small, but I'm not about to carry you."

He grunted, his lips pulled back from his teeth from the pain. "Not making...any promises."

The woman looked at Dakota. "All of our medical supplies are gone. Do you have anything we can use to help him?"

"We have water and some basic first aid in our bags," Logan said as he peered over Dakota's shoulder. "I'll get them and bring Shay."

"Hurry," Dakota said. "You need medical attention, too."

As he jogged off, the woman met Dakota's gaze. Wisps of ash-blonde hair clung to her temples, the rest of it yanked back in a tight bun.

"You saved our lives." She removed her mask and safety goggles, careful not to touch her reddened, sweaty face with her gloved hands.

In her late forties, she was a sturdy, broad-shouldered woman with a heavy jaw and a wide forehead, a spray of freckles spanning her weathered cheeks.

Dakota nodded tightly, momentarily forgetting about the goose egg swelling the right side of her head. A fresh wave of pain radiated across her skull, down her neck. She winced.

"I'm Nancy Harlow," the woman said. "Everyone calls me Harlow."

"Dakota Sloane."

The man only grunted.

"This is Yu-Jin Park," Harlow said, hooking her thumb at him. "I just call him Park."

"I apologize...for my lack of manners," he said through gritted teeth.

"I'm a security guard, or gaming surveillance officer if you will, at Hialeah Park Casino in Hialeah. Park works the tables as a poker dealer. The man loves gambling so much he made it his job. He has a temper on him, too, in case you didn't notice."

"They...started it," Park said.

Harlow rolled her eyes. "We met eight years ago during our smoking breaks, and we've been fast friends ever since. When I took the Emergency Medical Responder certification three years ago, he tagged along. He's an adrenaline junkie, is what he is. Jumps out of airplanes in his free time. Can you imagine? Who would jump out of a perfectly good plane?"

Dakota just stared at her.

Harlow didn't even seem to notice. She jabbered on, unfazed, almost manically calm. Like she was determined to carry on a regular conversation as if her life depended on it. Or maybe it was her sanity.

Dakota felt like she was barely holding on to sanity herself. Her hands were still trembling, no matter how hard she balled them into fists.

She hadn't lied to Logan. She didn't feel an ounce of guilt for killing Tank. But Logan was still right. Killing another human being, even someone who deserved it, always took something from you.

Three times she'd killed now. The ghost of her first kill still haunted her. Would this one? In her mind's eye, she kept seeing the jerk of the thug's head, the tiny spray of red mist, the way his dead marble eyes remained open after he'd died, staring straight through her. Just like Jacob's had.

She blinked back the terrible images and forced herself to focus on the present. No time for those thoughts now.

"Anyway," Harlow continued, "after the attacks, it only made sense to volunteer. I've only got my two cats at home, and my apartment is well clear of the hot zone, so they're fine as rain. Park and I are both single and childless, so..."

"Who better to volunteer...for radiation poisoning?" Park wheezed.

Dakota glanced at her watch. It was already 6:22 p.m. The sun had begun its descent across a sky hazy with distant fires. The humid air still smelled burnt. Her back prickled with heat.

How much radiation had their bodies soaked up in the last six hours? One gray, at least. Maybe as much as one and a half. They were past the initial threshold for acute radiation sickness themselves.

Her clothes should have protected her from the ground contamination during the fight, and she'd been careful not to touch her skin. It was Logan who'd exposed himself the most.

The side of her skull pulsed with pain, but that was from the blow to the head. She didn't feel any different—other than sore, tired, and hot, her limbs heavy beneath the weight of constant anxiety and fear.

They'd done their best with what they had, but radiation was an insidious, invisible poison they couldn't feel or see, even as it invaded their flesh, their bones, their internal organs. Not until it was far too late.

They hadn't even reached Eden yet, still an eternal half mile northwest.

She was so close. Dakota still felt like a vast canyon separated her from her sister. Her chest squeezed like a winch winding tighter and tighter.

Everything would be okay once she found her sister. Eden was her focus point, the thing that let her blot out everything else—the exhaustion, the fear, the dull horror of the fight and its aftermath seeping into her bones.

She looked up as Logan strode back toward the gas station. Shay and Julio trailed behind him, Julio still steadying Shay with his arm slung around her waist.

Shay pushed him gently away. "I'll be fine now."

Julio handed Harlow several sealed bottles of water, while Shay pulled a handful of fresh packages of gauze and medical tape out of Julio's sequined bag.

"Wash yourself," Dakota said to Logan. "Use the alcohol wipes."

She was concerned about him. It surprised her a little, but she didn't have time to think about it. She watched as Logan grabbed a couple of waters and flushed out his eyes, then wiped down every inch of his exposed skin with the wipes.

Julio helped Shay sink down beside Dakota and Harlow. She introduced herself as a nursing student. "May I take a look?"

"By all means," Harlow said, moving aside. "Here. I've got extra gloves." She dug into the medical bag tucked beneath Park's feet and pulled out two pairs of plastic, disposable gloves. Shay took one pair, Dakota the other.

Shay bent over Park and touched his uninjured shoulder gently. "Are you hurt anywhere other than your arm?"

"Just...my head."

"He smacked it against that metal pole," Dakota explained.

"I'm going to do a quick assessment, okay?" She examined him swiftly, checking his vital signs, his pulse and breathing. "His level of responsiveness is good. He's aware and able to communicate. But his pulse is low. His breathing rate is ten breaths a minute, also a bit low."

Her gaze dropped to his bloody, injured arm. She didn't flinch. Her expression remained calm and capable.

"Give it to me...straight, Doc," Park muttered.

"I'm not a doctor," she said with a tight smile. "But I can still help you, okay? You've got an open fracture. Looks like both the ulna and the radius are broken."

"We're going to have to try and set the bones, Park," Harlow said.

Park blanched. "No freakin' way."

"Yes," Shay said. "We've got to set the bones or you risk permanent damage with every movement. Plus, I need to irrigate the laceration to flush out the dirt and bacteria, then splint it."

"Please tell me you know how to do all that," Harlow said. "This is beyond my pay grade."

"Yes, though not outside of a medical setting." She glanced at Dakota. Dakota nodded back at her. "But I can do this."

"Oh, thank heavens," Harlow said. "That wasn't covered in our two-day training. I was going to make it up as I went along."

Park gritted his teeth. "Think I'm gonna just...pass out now."

"I think I might, too." Julio's face was tinged a sickly shade of green. He shuffled back toward Logan, shaking his head.

"We've got this," Shay said with confidence. "We just need the materials to make the splint."

"Ugh." Park's eyes rolled back in his head for a moment. "Just do it...fast."

"I saw a couple of short, broken pipes in the debris by the third gas pump," Dakota offered. "Maybe a foot long, half an inch thick?

And we can cut off the straps from one of our bags. It's almost empty anyway."

It was the bag that held their bottled waters—they were almost out.

"Perfect," Shay said as she gathered her supplies. Dakota found the pipes, scrubbed them free of contamination with several alcohol wipes, and cut the straps of a bag with her knife.

Shay told Park to wriggle his fingers. He did, but only slightly.

She frowned. "You could have pinched nerves or punctured blood vessels, or both. Once we set the bones, we'll try again."

"What now?" Dakota asked. They needed to get this done as fast as possible. She felt every second ticking by with agonizing slowness.

"We need to provide gentle traction to keep the bone ends apart and minimize pain as we splint the arm."

"That sounds...like torture," Park wheezed. "Please tell me you... have a tranquilizer in that bag."

"Sorry," Shay said. "We've got to do this the old-fashioned way."

3 2

DAKOTA

Dakota watched as Harlow helped Shay stabilize the fracture. Shay blinked several times. Her eyes were red and bloodshot.

"You okay?" Dakota asked.

"Stupid contacts," Shay muttered. "I've never wanted glasses so bad in my life."

"You're about to move my broken bones around...and you can't see?" Even more blood drained from Park's face.

Shay's jaw tightened. "I've got this. Don't worry."

"You ready?" Harlow asked Park.

"Absolutely not."

"Just pretend it's another thrill like leaping out of an airplane at twelve thousand feet. You like to live dangerously. Imagine the story you can tell all our co-workers."

"Go to hell," Park mumbled.

"You first. Steady now. Here comes the hard part."

Shay's hands were perfectly steady. She kept the jagged bone ends still by holding his arm above and below the fracture and exerting gentle traction in opposite directions.

"Son of a motherless—!"

Park cussed a blue streak, but Shay didn't even flinch. "Hold still or it will hurt more."

Harlow held his upper arm while Shay pulled gently on the lower arm below the break. Park groaned, the tendons standing out in his neck.

Slowly, the broken bones fitted back into place. His deformed forearm straightened.

Park squeezed his eyes shut, whimpering between gritted teeth. He didn't pass out, though he probably wanted to.

Harlow patted his healthy shoulder. "That wasn't so bad, was it?"

Park murmured an unintelligible response.

While Shay kept the arm immobilized, she walked Dakota through the process of caring for the puncture wound. Dakota irrigated the laceration carefully, dried the undamaged flesh with gauze, then covered it with a sterile dressing.

"For the splint, he needs something soft for padding so the metal pipes don't rub painfully against his skin," Shay said.

"How about we remove his PPE suit and cut it into strips?" Julio offered. "He won't be digging around in the rubble, so surface contamination shouldn't be an issue before he gets out of the hot zone."

"He's been lying on the ground," Dakota said. "The suit is contaminated. If we washed it, it would be wet against his skin. Seems like that's not the best option."

"True. Luckily, I have a spare shirt." Shay pointed to her bag, which Julio wore slung over his shoulder. "In Old Navy, I packed an extra just in case."

"Good thinking, Shay." Dakota and Harlow held Park still while Shay gently wrapped the bright pink long-sleeved shirt around his injured arm.

"Sorry it's pink," Shay said.

"My...favorite color."

They placed one of the pipes against either side of Park's arm and tied the straps of the shoulder bag just below his wrist and above his elbow to keep the break stabilized.

"Now, wriggle your fingers," Shay instructed.

They barely twitched.

Shay touched his fingertips. "Can you feel that?"

"Through the...pulsing agony? Not really."

Shay's frown deepened. "We need to get him to an experienced surgeon."

"Let's go, then," Dakota said.

"First, we need to make sure everyone else is okay." Shay stood, leaning against Dakota for balance, and surveyed the rest of the group. "You're bleeding," she said to Logan. "Let me see."

Logan stood with his back to one of the poles, pistol in hand, half-listening while keeping watch for any other dangers. The midsection of his black shirt was wet with blood.

He gave a weary shake of his head. "I'm fine."

"Like hell you are," Dakota said.

She'd seen the ugly gash across his ribs when he'd lifted his shirt earlier to check his injuries. It didn't look lethal, but it probably hurt like hell.

"You must have misheard me." Shay stepped toward him, swaying only slightly, and brandished the Neosporin at him. Her mouth was set in stubborn determination. "That wasn't a request."

Logan tensed. Dakota expected him to argue further, but he simply lifted his shirt with his free hand and let out a resigned sigh. Shay could be quite persuasive when she put her mind to it.

His abs and chest were lean but muscled. A dozen faint white scars crisscrossed his bronze skin. A purple bruise marred his left pectorals; another shadowed his right hip.

Logan saw her looking and flashed a tight grin.

She jerked her gaze away, her cheeks warming for some ridiculous reason.

Shay didn't even blink. She cleaned up the laceration, smeared his scrapes with topical antibiotics, applied two large squares of fresh gauze, and wrapped his ribs with medical tape.

"There's no reason to risk serious infection when we don't need to," Shay said sternly. "That's what I'm here for." She turned to Dakota. "Your turn."

Shay checked her pulse, her breathing, and her head, prodding with gentle fingers. Shay made Dakota follow her finger with her eyes. "Your pupils are fine. Any dizziness, confusion, ringing in your ears, nausea?"

"Nope." Dakota's skull felt like someone had nailed it with a hammer, which was close enough to the truth. But Shay didn't think she'd suffered a concussion.

They'd escaped rather unscathed, considering.

Except for Park.

"Can we get out of here now?" She rose to her feet, too anxious to keep still any longer. Her entire body was a bundle of nerves strung taut. All she could think of was Eden.

Julio wheeled over the all-terrain stretcher with oversized, eighteen-inch wheels.

"Pick him up gently and keep him in the recovery position," Shay instructed. "His vital signs need to be checked every five minutes. He's at risk for shock. Can you do that, Julio?"

"Happy to finally be useful," Julio said ruefully.

Together, Julio, Harlow, and Dakota carefully lifted Park, then loaded him onto the stretcher. He hissed out a pained breath with every shift and bump. Harlow elevated his legs again with her medical bag at the foot of the stretcher.

"Where's the nearest operational hospital?" Shay asked.

"Hialeah Hospital and Palmetto to the west and Coral Cables

and Doctors Hospital to the south are already inundated," Harlow said. "Jackson Memorial, North Shore, and Aventura had to be evacuated. Kendall Regional set up emergency triage tents in their parking lots, but they're flooded beyond capacity, too. We need to get him to—"

A loud beep shattered the stillness.

33
EDEN

Eden smelled something.

She sniffed again. It was still there.

She opened her eyes in the pitch-blackness, blinking hard.

She'd barely moved the last several hours. Her limbs felt heavy, like they were weighed down with cement.

Her muscles were stiff, her back and shoulders sore from two days lying in the tub, even with the cushions.

Her throat burned with thirst. Her mouth felt dry as a desert.

She'd been lost in a restless sleep, dreaming of monsters again, crouched and waiting, ready to pounce from the darkened corners of her mind.

Her empty, knotted stomach lurched with a wave of nausea.

She turned her head and spat. Only a few strings of saliva dribbled out.

She wiped her mouth with the back of her arm and sat up. She inhaled deeply, taking in the fetid stench that hung in the air. It was different than the acidic stink of urine from the toilet.

This smelled like rotten eggs.

From the fridge? But no. The fridge didn't have electricity, but it was sealed. There shouldn't be any smells escaping from it.

Could she be so hungry that she was smelling imaginary food? If that were the case, surely she'd smell delicious scrambled eggs or eggs-over-easy, or better yet, decadent roasted turkey or freshly baked cinnamon buns...

This was different. The stench was like rotten eggs, but also like something else she'd smelled before.

Last summer, Gabriella and Jorge had taken her to Florida Bay, which had stunk so bad she'd begged them to leave.

Jorge had explained the smell was hydrogen sulfide, produced by the natural decomposition in organic-rich marine mud. Something about the large amounts of organic material combined with low oxygen concentrations.

The explanation had gone over her head, except for the part about how small amounts of sulfide gas were added to propane gas so people could smell it in case of a gas leak in their home.

It was gas she smelled.

Gas leaking from somewhere inside the house.

She clambered to her feet, stepped out of the tub, and felt along the toilet and the counter to the sink.

She flipped the handles. Still no water. The sink was still bone dry.

A helpless sob ripped through her, wracking her ribs, choking her throat. She clutched the edges of the counter, staring into a mirror she couldn't see, trying not to panic.

But the panic was coming for her anyway, just like the monsters of her nightmares, the monsters who'd stolen her voice, who came creeping back every night, seeking the only thing they hadn't yet taken—her life.

Something terrible was coming, and she couldn't stop it by herself.

She wanted to scream and shout for someone to come and rescue her.

She opened her mouth, but only that terrible rasping breath came out—a mangled, ruined sound that no one would hear outside of the tomb of this awful, claustrophobic bathroom.

Her eyes stung. Tears leaked down her cheeks. Her chest hitched as she tried to hold back the waves of fear and worry and doubt.

Eden was afraid to stay. But she was terrified to leave.

Indecision gripped her.

She was used to other people telling her what to do—her real father, Maddox, then Dakota and Ezra, her social worker, now her foster parents.

Other people made the decisions, and she was content to follow. But now there was no one to give her direction.

No one to tell her which choice was the correct one, which led to suffering and death and which led to life.

She needed Dakota. She needed her sister.

Instead, she was stuck here, crying and scared like a little kid, alone in the silence and the dark.

And the leaking gas.

34

DAKOTA

Instinctively, Dakota tightened her grip on the Sig, heart hammering in her throat.

Logan dropped into a defensive posture. He kept his pistol in the low ready position and scanned the area warily.

Dakota did the same, taking in the sagging, debris-strewn gas station, the hunched, empty buildings, the desolate street.

Heat shimmered off the asphalt. Fifty yards ahead, several palm trees clumped in the island in the center of the street sagged listlessly. Humidity hung thick and heavy in the stagnant, smoky air.

No movement. No people. No threats other than the fires burning in the distance. Nothing she could see, anyway.

"Oh, sorry," Harlow said sheepishly. "That's just the alarm from my PERD, my Personal Emergency Radiation Detector."

"Your PPE suits don't protect you from gamma rays," Dakota said. With the attack and its aftermath, she'd forgotten the first responders were willingly exposing themselves to radiation, too. "How long have you been out here?"

Harlow tapped a small black pager-like object attached to a flap of her suit. "We're monitoring our dosage. The alarm means we've surpassed our safety limits. Each unit takes turns with limited time in the hot zone. Our unit already went back, but we two geniuses decided to try and rescue one more person since we still had the stretcher."

"Turns out...that was a horrible idea," Park grunted.

"We were assigned to one of the initial triage sites set up at Miami Jordan High School off 36th Street, the nearest casualty collection point for evacuees and the injured." Harlow frowned. "But they don't have the resources to care for Park."

"That double fracture requires surgery," Shay warned, "or his arm will be deformed permanently. There's a pinched or torn nerve. He could lose complete use of his hand."

Harlow nodded grimly. "We need to go to the airport."

Park squeezed his eyes shut. "That's too far. I'll die from the pain...before we ever get there."

"No, you won't, you big baby." Harlow shook her head. "My favorite cousin is an ER doctor at Miami North Medical Center. It suffered damage from the blast, so she's been reassigned to the EOC to oversee triage. She can get us admitted, then get you on the priority list for medical evac. This isn't a choice, Park, so stop whining."

She turned to Dakota and the others to explain. "They've shut down Miami International—except for medical, government, and military flights—and turned it into the regional Emergency Operations Center.

"They sectioned off a huge part of the domestic terminal for emergency medical triage and treatment for injuries and radiation victims. They're also coordinating medical evacuations to the nearest regional hospitals accepting patients, some over a hundred miles away."

Harlow glanced at Shay's bandaged head, at their sweat-stained, duct-taped long-sleeved shirts and pants, the scarves draping their necks.

"You should get that head wound checked out yourself," she said. "And you've got to get out of the hot zone. We're a mile straight west from the contamination border. You should come to the EOC with us."

Dakota swallowed. "We will, but I need to find my sister. She's only a half mile from here. Shay, you're welcome to go with them."

"I will as soon as I can," Shay said. "But if it's all the same, I'd see Dakota reunited with her sister first. She saved all of our lives by getting us to a safe shelter."

Heat spread up Dakota's throat and burned her cheeks. Was that the real reason Shay had insisted on coming with them—to help Dakota in repayment for saving her life?

Dakota hadn't done it for thanks or accolades or favors owed. It wasn't like that. "You don't owe me anything."

Shay gave her a warm smile. "That's where you're wrong."

Julio turned to Harlow. "There's a group of survivors at the Showtime 14 cinema in Overtown in auditorium seven. And another group sheltering in place at the Palm Industries Center building west of Wynwood. Could you send a team in to rescue them?"

Harlow nodded. "I'll radio it in and relay the information to our team leader. They'll do what they can, I promise. If those people are still there, we'll get them out."

"Thank you," Shay said.

The woman hesitated. She glanced down at Park, then eyed Dakota and Logan's weapons and pursed her lips. Her eyes were wide, her pupils huge. "What if we came with you? A half mile isn't too far out of the way, right, Park?"

"Why don't you just go to South Beach...while you're at it?" he said. "Don't worry about me...in agony over here...about to go into shock and die."

She patted his uninjured arm. Her hand was trembling. "That's just the pain talking. He's normally very agreeable."

"Nope," Park muttered. "Pretty sure I'm not."

Harlow ignored him. She turned to Dakota and Logan. "The attack set back our timetable. We're too far from the EOC or the established triage sites to reach them by sundown."

For the first time, the woman's brisk, unflappable mask slipped. She looked terrified. She cleared her throat, then cleared it again. "To tell the honest truth, I'm worried about more crazies coming out of the woodwork, you know?

"We thought...we thought for sure no one would bother first responders. Not in the hot zone, not during the day. Who would do something like that?"

No one said anything.

"The world's gone crazy on us." Harlow's voice cracked. The unnatural calm was gone. Her face was pale, her solid jaw clenched. "It's like we've been overrun by zombies. Those people who came at us were...evil. Pure evil."

Her features contorted. Her whole body was trembling. But it wasn't in fear or shock—it was anger. "I volunteered to help people, damn it! Just being out here, I'm increasing my cancer risk by over thirty percent. Maybe more, I don't want to know. We risked our lives! And for what? Those people...those people would've killed us for nothing, for our masks, or maybe just...just because."

She looked down at Park and sucked in a sharp breath. "If they had killed Park...This was my idea. He went into the hot zone because of me. He's a good person. Annoying and stubborn as all hell, but good. Not like them. Those ungrateful savages."

"Most people aren't like that," Julio said. "I believe the majority of people want to do the decent thing and treat each other right."

"Not from where I'm standing." The skin across Harlow's knuckles whitened over her clenched fists. "I believed the same as you. Hell, I was one of the first volunteers. I was a fool. And it almost cost Park his life.

"No more," she growled through gritted teeth. "I'm just taking care of me and my own now."

Dakota was hard-pressed to disagree with her. The veneer of civilization was just a mask. She had seen behind that mask often enough.

Maybe there were a few good people in the world, but most of them were only out for themselves. Maybe they wouldn't resort to violence as quickly as these scumbags had, who'd been driven by pain and panic and radiation poisoning.

But hunger would do the same thing. And fear.

"We weren't...ready," Park said. "For this."

"No one is ready," Julio said. "But we're doing the best we can."

Dakota intended to do better than that. She pulled her new Sig out and rested it against her thigh, just in case. There were five bullets left. She wrapped her hand around the comforting grip. She'd missed this.

Never again. The knife wasn't enough. She'd never go without a weapon. She needed the gun. She desperately needed the reassuring feeling of *no one will ever hurt you again*.

"You're okay, now." Shay shot Dakota a hopeful look. "You're with us."

"It's the right thing to do." Julio touched his cross. "We can't just leave them. We were headed toward Miami International anyway."

Harlow took a shuddering breath. For a moment, her face slackened, but then she seemed to regain control of herself, though her eyes still flashed with anger. "We would appreciate that."

Dakota closed her eyes for a second against the throbbing pain in her head. The eerie silence pressed in on her, the heat sapping her little remaining energy.

Another wounded person would slow them down further. But Julio was right. She couldn't turn her back now. They couldn't just leave a woman by herself with a helpless guy on a stretcher at night in a lawless city.

"Maybe I should just run ahead and get Eden myself," Dakota said. "It's only half a mile."

"Are you insane?" Julio asked. "We've already been attacked twice today! And I didn't even count hiding while four thugs with assault rifles hunted us! No one should go anywhere alone out here, not until we get to the EOC and back to civilization."

"And you shouldn't be running anywhere with that knot on your head," Shay warned. "A concussion is still a possibility. You need to take it easy."

Dakota blew out a frustrated breath.

It went against every fiber of her being not to take off running right now.

They were close to Eden. Maybe only thirty minutes to an hour, depending on the fires and other obstacles in their path. Then it was just a mile out of the hot zone.

They might not be safe yet, but at least she'd have her sister and they'd be free of the radiation threat.

She glanced at Logan. He dipped his chin slightly in agreement.

The dull glassiness in his gaze was gone. He was sharp and alert, but there were still shadows behind his eyes. He looked like a man haunted.

She'd watched him dump his flask after the fight. Did that mean he was done with being a drunk? How did that change things?

Logan had fought well despite his drinking. They'd beaten off the psychos together. They made a decent team. Together, they could protect Eden and themselves from whatever threats awaited them between here and their destination.

As a security guard, Harlow knew her way around a gun, too. And what if Eden was hurt? Shay could help her. Plus, there was safety in numbers.

It would be stupid to go it alone, even if it was faster.

Her mind made up, Dakota holstered her Sig but kept her palm resting on the butt. Now, she was prepared. "We'll all go together. And then we'll escort you two to the EOC. But we have to move."

3 5

LOGAN

Logan and Dakota strode just ahead of the group, clearing the path of debris and keeping an eye out for hostiles.

Dakota had the Sig; Logan his Glock. Harlow agreed to carry the M4, though she said she preferred her Smith and Wesson 642 revolver. Unfortunately, it was back at her condo with her cats.

Julio had offered to push the stretcher. Shay walked on one side, her hand on the stretcher to keep her steady, while Harlow took the other side, constantly checking on Park's vitals. Park lay rigid, grimacing and hissing with every jolt. His right arm was splinted from his elbow to his wrist.

The heat lessened as the sun slid slow and languid across the sky, but the air was still thick, heavy with smoke from the fires surging in the distance. The humidity was stifling as a wool blanket against his skin.

They continued along Bay Point Drive toward Palm Cove, Bellview Court, and Dakota's sister.

Small one-story stucco houses in shades of pastel yellow, burnt orange, and faded coral crowded together on tiny, brown-grass lots.

Broken glass littered porches and walkways. Every door was shut, blinds and curtains closed.

The street was completely still. No cars honking. No children yelling and shrieking. No music playing or cellphones ringing. The only sounds were the squeak of the stretcher's wheels and their own footsteps and ragged breaths.

No crashed cars blocked the road here, though most of the vehicles were gone. A few leftovers were parked along the curb or sat in short driveways.

A burgundy Nissan Versa had both front doors flung open, as if its frantic owners changed their minds mid-getaway and abandoned the Versa for a better option.

A purple tricycle with sparkling teal streamers lay on its side on one yard; in another, an inflated baby pool filled with water collected pine needles from a nearby slash pine tree.

The air smelled of mown grass and car exhaust—and the singed stink of smoke and burnt plastic. The smoke stench seemed heavier, thicker. He could taste it in the back of his throat.

A flash of movement caught his eye. In the broken front window of a squat, eggshell-blue house, the blinds gently swayed.

Someone was watching them.

He tightened his two-handed grip on the Glock and spun in a slow circle, scanning the area, taking in everything. Nothing else moved. The street remained quiet.

There were still people living in the tiny house, sheltering in place, but with hardly any protection from the deadly gamma rays.

How many families were still here, hidden and cowering with their children, blindly hoping they'd made the right decision?

He lowered the gun, still holding it in one hand, and ran his other hand gingerly over his ribs, wincing. He glanced back at the purple tricycle, those sparkling teal streamers.

Hot anger ran through him like an electrical current. He flexed his stinging knuckles. He wanted to strangle whoever was responsible, to smash their teeth in with his bare fists. To hurt and be hurt.

The back of his throat burned. He felt it like a pressure growing behind his eyes. He wanted a damn drink.

He wasn't going to get one. Not now, not ever.

"What can you tell us about what's going on?" he asked between gritted teeth, desperate for a distraction. "What is the government doing to help?"

"The government as we know it is gone. It'll take months for them to get on their feet again. I don't know how much they were helping the little people before, but they're sure gonna be useless now."

"What do you mean?" Shay asked.

"Our response organizations are woefully underprepared," Harlow said. "Medical staff and first responders can hardly communicate with each other, let alone the public. We're severely lacking in resources and manpower. We experienced a huge loss of first responders in the blast—hundreds of firefighters, police officers, EMTs, nurses, and doctors.

"A lot of people evacuated; others left their posts to care for their families. I don't blame them. Heck, if I had family, they'd be my first priority, too. It is what it is. We're all doing the best we can. I haven't slept in thirty-six hours. Neither have most of the people on our team."

"What about the radiation?" Shay asked.

"Millions fled the fallout," Harlow said. "Even in unaffected cities, people panicked and tried to escape. The entire country is a mess. Within five minutes of the first bomb, cell coverage and even the internet got so overloaded, nothing worked.

"It didn't matter. Even though the emergency alerts went out over all the radio channels, people panicked anyway. They relied on gut instinct and fear—instead of following instructions, they dropped everything and ran."

Park winced as the stretcher bumped over a pothole. "Not like instructions...did any good here."

Harlow's face darkened. "Governor Blake based the entire regional response plan on the cigar-shaped Gaussian fallout pattern in all the nuclear disaster planning literature. Apparently, he thought the radiation would only affect a symmetrical, easily-defined area. He was dead wrong."

Dakota nodded. "In the real world, fallout patterns are irregular."

"Think post-modern art," Park wheezed.

Harlow sidestepped a silver Ford Fiesta parked at the curb at a forty-five-degree angle. One of the rear passenger doors hung open, two pink car seats stuffed in the back.

"He sent out emergency broadcasts instructing entire neighborhoods that were safer sheltering in place to evacuate instead," she said angrily. "Blake always was an idiot. He gave them evacuation routes directly within the path of the fallout! People had no clue what to do!

"I knew the broadcasts were wrong as soon as I heard them. I was in the middle of dealing with a belligerent guest who'd just lost five grand at Blackjack when the emergency alert came over my comm. I told my co-workers—Park included—to stay put, and I tried to call all my friends and family, but the phones were already down. There was no way to warn anyone.

"Thousands of innocent people were trapped in their cars on US1. Every highway was clogged with bumper-to-bumper traffic with no way to escape the radiation."

Harlow balled her gloved hands into fists, her eyes flashing with helpless rage. "Such a waste of human life. A tragedy of ineptitude on a monumental scale. I hope Blake loses his job over this."

"Better yet...a lifetime appointment in prison," Park said.

"It's the least he could do," Harlow said.

Park grimaced. "Common sense is like deodorant...the people who need it most...never use it."

"He thinks he's Yoda."

"Don't cramp...my style," Park mumbled.

Logan suppressed a grim smile. He liked this guy already.

They turned off Bay Point Drive onto a side road.

"It's only a quarter mile to Eden," Dakota said as she lengthened her stride. Logan hurried to catch up.

"Dakota, you need to slow down," Shay said, but Dakota didn't seem to hear her.

"I thought the government would be prepared for something like this," Julio said.

Harlow snorted. "In theory. The Department of Health and Human Services does have a Strategic National Stockpile. They've got twelve designated units and classified points across the country with huge supplies of antibiotics, vaccines, gas masks, and IV solutions."

"Great," Shay said. "When will they get here?"

"They won't. They can't." Harlow blinked, holding back tears of exhaustion and frustration. "At least, not for a while. We've begged for aid, but how can they help? There are twelve other devastated cities."

"They triaged the cities," Park said. "Miami...didn't make the list."

"What about FEMA? The National Guard?" Julio asked.

Harlow only shook her head.

"What does that mean?" Logan asked.

Harlow stared at them bleakly. "We're on our own."

Logan felt like he'd been kicked in the chest. The ground

seemed to roll and buckle beneath him, like a sinkhole was about to crack open and swallow him up.

He glanced at Dakota. She strode beside him, silent and tense, her jaw set, her dark eyes flinty and unreadable.

"That can't be right," Shay murmured. "It must be a mistake."

"It's not," Harlow said flatly. "Oh, they've promised us help, but we're not the priority. It'll be days before any aid comes. Maybe weeks."

Dakota said the words no one wanted to hear. "Maybe longer."

For a long moment, no one spoke.

"Americans are strong," Shay said in a soft voice. "We're resilient. We're not gonna let anyone break us. Right?"

She looked at Logan and Dakota hopefully, her gaze pleading, desperate.

No one could answer that question. Not yet.

36

LOGAN

ogan ignored the burning in his throat, the *need* pulsing against his skull, and quickened his pace. He forced himself to concentrate on the conversation around him.

"Yoselyn, my wife, is in West Palm Beach," Julio said. "How far did the fallout cloud reach?"

"West Palm Beach is, what, seventy-five miles north?" Harlow asked. "The radiation didn't hit them. The news reported the plume drifted almost sixty miles north and west all the way to Boynton Beach, radiating everything between the coast and the Everglades north of Fort Lauderdale."

"All of which is uninhabitable now?" Shay asked softly.

Harlow tightened her grip on the side of Park's stretcher. "For a while, anyway. All those schools, hospitals, factories, refineries, and businesses no one can use now. Multiply that by thirteen."

"That's...hard to imagine," Julio said.

"There was a frantic run on the banks within an hour of the attack. Now every bank in the country is closed. I can't pull out anything from the ATMs. The stores still open are cash only. Luckily, I had a few hundred dollars for a sofa I was planning to buy on Craigslist. Who carries money around anymore?

"With Wall Street destroyed in New York City, there's no NASDAQ or New York Stock Exchange. Every other exchange plummeted so steeply within a couple minutes of opening, they've closed them all."

"What does that mean?" Logan asked with a sickening feeling in his gut. "Long-term."

Harlow shook her head. "Your guess is as good as mine."

"It means the end of the world...as we know it," Park said, grimacing. "Cue the music."

"Cue you shutting up," Harlow said, not unkindly. "You need to conserve your energy, not blabber on about useless predictions. *No one* knows. That's the point."

"Do you have a phone on you by chance?" Julio asked. "I just want to hear her voice. I need to know she's safe, you know?"

"I'd love to help you, but I can't," Harlow said. "I've only had coverage twice in the last fifty-six hours, and only for a few seconds or so. Towers are so overloaded, no one can connect. No calls are going through. Maybe a text message if you're lucky."

Julio's face fell. "So even after we get out of the EMP range, we won't be able to call our loved ones?"

"Millions of people are in the dark," Park said. "Literally and figuratively."

"What do you mean?" Logan asked.

"Rolling power outages are widespread in a lot of places," Harlow explained. "Some in states that weren't even hit. A bunch of substations were damaged in the blasts. Others are located in the hot zone and had to be evacuated. At least Governor Blake claims everything will be back online in several days."

"No." Julio shook his head. "I've read about this. Those large boilers, turbines, and transformers are custom-made. It'll take months to repair. The electric grid is so interconnected that a few lost substations could cause extended blackouts over several states."

"Fantastic," Harlow said bitterly. "Our illustrious governor is wrong again."

Park shifted on the stretcher, wincing. "Or lying to us...that butt-ugly moron."

Logan glanced at Dakota. Everything she'd said back in the theater about the potentially devastating ripple effects were already coming true.

Everything depended on power. What would happen if huge regions of the country were forced to struggle without it for weeks or months?

Coupled with the enormous nuclear disasters, could it be enough to bring the entire country to its knees?

Maybe they really would need that safehouse after all.

His breath quickened. He forced himself to focus on the here and now, on every step and breath and beat of his heart.

It was the only way he knew how to get through this moment and the next, and the next. One damned thing at a time.

"Do we know who did this yet?" he asked.

"The CIA, FBI, and Homeland are chasing down leads, but they haven't reported anything yet," Harlow said. "Homeland Security is working with the Nuclear Regulatory Commission to investigate the source of the highly enriched uranium used in the bombs. But honestly, I've been out here every spare second bringing in survivors. I'm not as up-to-date as I should be. I'm sure we'll find out more at the EOC."

"What's that?" Julio pointed east over their heads. "What happened there?"

A massive column of thick black smoke billowed into the sky above a cluster of nearby homes, much larger and darker than the hazy smoke they'd seen all day.

And closer.

"Whatever it is, it looks bad," Logan muttered.

"Another rescue unit retreated from that direction right before those crazies attacked us," Harlow said. "They had to evacuate early because a gas line broke in some gated community. A bunch of houses caught fire, just like that."

Beside him, Dakota halted abruptly.

Logan stopped and glanced down at her. "What is it?"

"What did you say?" Dakota asked Harlow.

"They cleared the area as best they could," Harlow said, "but there are hundreds of fires burning all over the city. We can't get fire trucks in with all the roads blocked by rubble."

"What subdivision?" Dakota asked in a strangled voice, her face drained of color. "What street?"

"I'm not sure, they all start to run together..."

"What street?!"

Tension twisted in Logan's own gut at the urgency in Dakota's voice, the desperation in her eyes.

"I remember," Park said. "Bellwether or something...I think—"

"Bellview?"

"Yes, that's it—"

Park didn't get to finish his sentence.

Without a word, Dakota broke into a sprint, running toward the rising pillar of black smoke.

37

DAKOTA

Dakota sprinted down the road toward the palm-lined side street that led to the Palm Cove gated community, her legs pumping, pulse racing.

Even in the heat, her veins turned to ice, cold terror flushing through every cell in her body.

She heard voices behind her, yelling at her to stop, their shouting shattering the thick, eerie silence.

She didn't slow down. She couldn't.

She hadn't prayed in years, but she prayed now. She recited the same two urgent sentences again and again in her mind: *Please be there. Please be safe. Please be there. Please be safe.*

Her heart closed like a fist, clenching tighter and tighter with each pounding footfall. The fear she'd been holding at bay all this time struck her now with a blind panic.

She'd told Eden to hole up and stay inside no matter what. If the house caught fire, she might be trapped or overcome by smoke inhalation.

Eden wouldn't be able to speak or scream or call out for help.

If something happened to Eden, it was because of her. It would be her fault...

It's too late.

No. It couldn't be too late. Dakota refused to accept that possibility.

Her breath came in ragged gasps, the thick, smoky air clogging in her throat and stinging her nostrils.

Her swollen scalp felt like it would burst from the pain. Her weary thigh muscles burned.

But she wouldn't slow down, not for anything.

She pushed on, panting, clutching at her side. *Come on, come on. Run faster, damn it!*

And then, finally, the Palm Cove gated community appeared ahead of her, clusters of regal palm trees surrounding the pompous "welcome" signage and high stucco walls, the wrought-iron gate at the guard station hanging wide open.

She sprinted past the empty station, dashed through the gate, and turned off the main road, running across several manicured lawns.

She dodged between two houses, barely noticing the tumbled lanai furniture; the pools littered with blown debris, elephant palm leaves, shredded shrubs and flowers; the screen over a paved lanai half-collapsed across a brick outdoor kitchen.

She scrambled over a fallen portion of white plastic picket fence, skirted a large manmade pond, and broke through a row of chest-high bushes into the backyards of the stately homes lining Bellview Court.

Fire consumed several houses, windows and roofs blazing, black smoke pouring into the air. The acrid stench seared Dakota's nostrils and the back of her throat.

Coughing frantically, she pressed her scarf tighter over her nose and mouth as she ran.

The back of Eden's house came into view. She recognized it

from the Google Earth imaging she'd done when Eden first smuggled her the address.

It was a big, tan two-story house with powder-blue shutters and a Spanish tile roof.

Cultivated roses and magnolias rimmed the massive covered lanai. Large ceramic pots sprawling with some kind of purple and white flowers framed the huge pool, the water still sparkling and vivid blue.

It was beautiful except for the shattered windows and broken French doors—and the roaring flames licking the window sills.

Her heart jerked, bucking against her rib cage.

Eden was in there. The only thing that mattered.

Panic clawed at her throat. She forced her frenetic thoughts to focus. *Think!* Be smart.

Where would Eden hide? Where would Dakota hide, if it were her?

The center of the house, no windows, on the first floor to escape the radiation penetrating the roof, just like Ezra had taught them.

A bathroom.

She imagined the layout the way Eden had described it. A large, open kitchen and living and dining areas to the right—that's where the fire burned. The master bedroom sprawled at the other end of the house on the left, along with some offices, guest rooms, and a theater room. Three more bedrooms were located upstairs.

She jerked the bent lanai screen door. Locked. Whipping out her knife, she slashed the screen with a single swift motion and scooted inside.

At the French doors, she hesitated. A blast of heat struck her, solid as a wall. Ribbons of smoke writhed through the air. Every breath she inhaled singed her throat. Her eyes watered.

Fear stuck like a hook in her belly. Her chest tightened, her throat closing, cutting off her breath.

In an instant, it all came back.

The scars on her back smoldered like they were fresh burns. The memories seared through her—the hiss of the white-hot embers as they branded her skin, the stench of her own charred flesh, the tormented shrieks of agony wrenched from her anguished throat.

Maddox leaning over her, that sharp, ravenous look in his eyes, his lip curled in twisted delight. *Are we not merciful? Fire is judgment...fire is mercy...only fire burns away the impurities of the flesh...*

She hated fire. Feared it with all her being. Every cell in her body screamed at her to stop, to turn around, to go back.

She squeezed her eyes shut, trying in vain to block out the boiling smoke, the crackling, seething flames.

It was Eden who'd sat with her each time after the mercy room.

It was Eden who sang comforting hymns in her sweet, soulful voice as Dakota lay on her bare belly on the bed, moaning and gripping handfuls of sheets so hard she ripped her nails.

It was Eden who bent over her raw, boiled back, who gently flushed the wounds, applied antibiotic gel, and dressed the weeping burns.

And it was Eden who refused to leave her side even once during the endless, agonizing nights.

I'll never leave you, Dakota had promised her in return. *Never, ever.*

This was her choice.

For her sister, she would brave anything, even if it meant being burned alive.

One, two, three. Breathe.

That's how you got through the hard stuff, Sister Rosemarie had told her after the first branding. That's how you endured.

Breathe, damn it, breathe!

She inhaled sharply. She opened her eyes.

Dakota stepped through the French doors.

3 8

DAKOTA

Intense heat blasted Dakota. She tightened the scarf over her nose and mouth, but it didn't matter.

Acrid smoke scorched her throat and lungs and she coughed, struggling not to choke as tears stung her eyes.

Smoke churned and boiled beneath the high ceilings, turning the house dark and hazy. Flames roared on Dakota's right, crackling and popping as it devoured the walnut cabinets, the chic Pottery Barn farm table, and the Brazilian hardwood flooring.

"Eden!" she screamed.

It came out like a croak. She cleared her throat as best she could and tried again.

"Eden! Where are you!"

She paused, trying to get her bearings. Stinging tears leaked from her eyes. The air was shimmering with heat, everything distorted like a desert mirage.

To her left, the breakfast nook seethed with noxious fumes. But it wasn't on fire. Not yet.

Directly ahead past the kitchen, she glimpsed white leather

sofas, a glass coffee table, and a glossy grand piano across from a huge picture window in the formal living room.

She turned to her left and staggered farther in, her hands out as she bumped against some weird tufted bench against the wall. She made her way past a pair of closed French doors leading to an office filled with black bookcases and an oversized desk.

And there, finally, was the hallway: long and narrow and filled with closed doors on either side.

Smoke curled along the ceiling ahead of her. She ducked to a crouch and felt the first closed door on her left, then the bronze handle—it was warm, not hot.

She opened the door to a home theater with six leather La-Z-Boy chairs and a giant screen, the walls decorated with old movie posters that had probably cost a fortune.

She moved on. Behind her, the fire was a crackling, popping cacophony, a pulsing roar in her ears.

Another door, a second office, this one sleek with metal and glass.

Double doors on her right led to a guest room with a bed nicer than any she'd slept in her entire life, a half-dozen plush, embroidered pillows scattered across the silky, coral-pink duvet.

It didn't matter. None of it mattered.

"Eden!" she shouted. "Show me where you are! I'm coming!"

Another hacking cough tore through her lungs, strangling her breath. Her brain screamed at her to get the hell out of there, but she couldn't. Not yet.

Already on her knees, she doubled over, gulping in scalding air devoid of oxygen her lungs so desperately needed. Waves of dizziness roiled through her. Darkness wavered at the corners of her vision.

She heaved, coughing violently, eyes bleeding tears. Barely able to see, she blinked furiously and rubbed the stinging wetness from her eyes.

How much longer did she have before the smoke overwhelmed her?

Not long. She could already feel it burning in her chest, her lungs.

There, just ahead of her. Another door.

She crawled on her hands and knees, wheezing, struggling for every breath, her lungs about to explode. She touched the wood, then the handle. Warm, not hot.

She pushed on the handle. The door didn't open immediately. Something on the other side hampered its movement. She shoved harder, straining with her exhausted arms. *Come on, come on!*

"Move!" she grunted desperately.

She pushed again, slamming her shoulder into the door.

She half-collapsed as it finally gave way against her weight.

She pushed the door open and crawled on her elbows into the small bathroom. At first she could barely see through the heavy shadows. It stank of piss, though she could barely smell anything over the acrid, stinging smoke.

There were no windows. A couple of large sofa cushions peeked out of the ivory claw-foot tub. Wedged beneath the door was a rumpled turquoise bath mat tangled with a fluffy towel—that's why she'd had trouble opening it.

Eden. She had to be here.

"Where are you! Answer me!" she cried even though she knew Eden couldn't respond.

She crawled deeper inside the bathroom, the tile unnaturally warm beneath her palms. She reached up to the marble counter and felt for standing water in the sink.

The first thing Ezra had taught them to do in a power outage or other emergency was to conserve water.

The sink was bone dry.

She moved to the tub and pushed aside the cushions in a desperate, futile hope that Eden would be lying there, grinning up at her, *Surprise!* scrawled in her little notepad.

The tub was empty.

Eden wasn't there.

3 9

DAKOTA

No, no, no!

Dakota hadn't survived a nuclear blast and journeyed across burning, radioactive Miami to lose everything now. This wasn't how it was supposed to go.

She'd done everything right! Everything she possibly could.

Eden was supposed to be here.

"Eden!" she croaked.

A dark shape at the bottom of the tub caught her eye.

Her sister's notepad.

Blinking fiercely, Dakota picked it up with trembling hands.

She smoothed the satiny surface of the unicorn leaping over the rainbow clouds, touched the drawing pencil neatly tucked into the spirals, pressed the pads of her fingers to the smooth, high-quality paper for sketching and drawing.

Dakota had bought it for Eden's fifteenth birthday a month ago. It was a copy of the one she'd bought last year, and the year before that.

Eden loved it, and when she loved something, she wanted it over and over—like macaroni and cheese, chocolate-covered rice crispy treats, or her favorite dystopian novels. Sometimes, she would wear the same shirt over and over until Dakota or Ezra forced her to wash it.

Eden never went anywhere without her notepad. It was her language, her way to express herself, to communicate.

It was her voice.

Her sister had been here.

But she'd left without her notepad.

What if she'd left the bathroom, searching for an escape from the smoke and the fire, and passed out somewhere, unable to cry for help?

Dakota's heart clenched. Dread seeped into every pore. Fear throbbed through her bones.

If she didn't find Eden right now, it would be too late.

Her sister trusted her. Depended on her.

Dakota would not fail her.

She had to check the rest of the house. Tucking the notepad down her shirt, Dakota slithered out of the bathroom on her belly, keeping her head as close to the floor as possible.

The air was gray, thick with ash, and hot. So hot, it felt like her skin was melting off her bones. Her eyebrows felt scorched.

A dull roar filled her ears. Black smoke roiled above her head, heaving and snarling like some monstrous creature.

Cotton stuffed her aching head. Her thoughts came jumbled and disconnected, the smoke and the strange house disorienting her.

Which way was she supposed to go?

Dazed and woozy, she managed to turn her head to her left. Her lethargic brain took far too long to process the sight before her.

Tongues of fire licked the walls only fifteen feet behind her in the hallway. Flames whooshed into the opened doorways she'd left behind, drawn by the oxygen sucked in through the shattered windows.

Stupid. She should've closed the doors. Too late now.

Not that way.

She turned slowly and crawled for the other end of the hall.

Her limbs felt so heavy, like they were weighed down with boulders. She was so tired. Every movement took phenomenal effort.

She reached another door but barely had the strength to reach up and open it.

Eden.

She could no longer speak the word aloud. Her parched tongue stuck to the roof of her bone-dry mouth.

Darkness fringed her vision. Unconsciousness was coming for her, hunting her.

It would be so easy to just give in, to let the cool, sweet darkness carry her away into oblivion.

Every terrible memory, gone. Every brand and burn, gone. Every person who'd ever betrayed her, gone. Maddox, the compound, the group home, her parents' death; all gone. The blood, the body—erased forever.

No more pain, no more suffering, no more horror...

How easy it would be. How simple. It would all go away. The fear, the anxiety, the guilt.

All she had to do was stop fighting. Give in. Give up on herself. On Eden.

Her thoughts fragmented, turning to ash, just bits of embers glowing in her feverish mind.

Give up.

No...Never.

Go to sleep.

Had to find...Eden.

It's so easy. The only easy thing you've ever done. Just close your eyes.

Couldn't...give up...

Never, ever.

40

DAKOTA

N*ever, ever.*

Through the hazy darkness of Dakota's muddled mind, a single ember glowed dimly. She was fading. Some part of her knew she was fading, knew this was it.

If she didn't get the hell up right this second, it would be over.

Dakota didn't give up. She didn't know how.

Her eyes fluttered. She moaned hoarsely.

A sound reached her, hazy and distant but closer, closer, jarring her dulled senses.

The snap and crackle of things bursting into flame—carpet, books, and magazines, lamps, throw pillows, and brocade curtains, wood and metal and plastic, filing cabinets and shelves, picture frames melting off the walls.

Slowly, painfully, she turned her head, blinking through the stinging tears, the thick haze of smoke.

The house was engulfed in flames. The fire blazed with a crackling, popping cacophony, a pulsing roar in her ears.

It surged down the hall after her, a devouring dragon desperate to breathe, to feed.

Sheer terror careened through her body. Drawing on the last of her energy, she forced herself to her elbows, wriggled frantically for the nearest door, and pushed it open.

She crawled blindly inside. She dragged herself all the way in, then, groaning, she twisted her body and kicked at the door.

It swung half-closed.

A wave of blistering heat swept toward her, followed on its heels by the ravenous fire. Flames darted through the doorway, seeking her with their scalding tongues.

Her skin felt roasted. Her eyebrows were singed. The stench of burning hair filled her nostrils.

Her tortured lungs dragged in a breath of scorched air. Maybe her last, if she didn't do something, if she couldn't find a way to get out of there, stop the fire somehow...

If she couldn't shut the damn door.

With a desperate, howling scream, she gathered her waning strength and kicked again. Her heel slammed against the heavy wood.

This time, the door banged shut.

She nearly cried with relief.

It was a moment of reprieve. It wouldn't last long.

Gasping, she flipped back onto her belly and dragged herself across the carpet. Her arms were so damn heavy. She could hardly lift her legs.

She was trapped in quicksand, her body constricted and sinking, sinking...

Come on! Move, damn it!

A dresser stood to her right. Beside it was an arched hallway leading to a large walk-in closet, the door slightly ajar. A huge king-sized bed in a massive whitewashed frame loomed directly ahead of her.

Dim light streamed into the master bedroom from somewhere over the bed. A window. She crawled toward it.

Sharp pricks stabbed her hands and forearms. Droplets of blood beaded her palms. Glass shards from the shattered windows littered the plush white carpet and the bed.

She sucked in a hoarse whimper and kept going.

She forced herself to her knees, enduring the sting of fresh cuts as more glass dug into her kneecaps. She tried to brush off her hands, but it was useless.

Several glass shards were embedded too deep. She couldn't afford the time it would take to pry them from her skin.

Using the bed frame, she pulled herself to her knees.

A wave of dizziness washed over her. Her head pounded from lack of oxygen, her heartbeat throbbing in her chest.

White stars danced and flickered in front of her eyes. She felt herself going limp, her muscles slackening, the dark oblivion descending again.

It was coming. This time, there was nothing she could do to stop it.

Her legs collapsed beneath her.

"Dakota!"

She flung out her hands to catch herself. The sharp sting of glass piercing deeper into her skin brought her back.

She fought the dark, forcing herself to open her eyes, blinking groggily.

"Dakota!"

The voice wasn't unconsciousness beckoning.

It was real.

She opened her mouth. Nothing came out. Panic gripped her.

This was how Eden felt—voiceless, vulnerable, powerless. Unable to communicate even the most basic tenet of human communication: *help.*

Gripping the bedpost, she pulled herself back up again, inch by painful inch. Bits of glass still clung to her arms, hands, and knees. With each movement, tiny needles jabbed her skin again and again. She winced and ignored them.

Orange, flickering fingers pried at the door behind her, smoke pouring in through the cracks as the fiery dragon roared to get in, to get to her. The air was blurry with heat, her eyes stinging so badly she could hardly see.

"Dakota!"

"I'm here!" she croaked.

She crawled on her knees for the window, coughing relentlessly, struggling for each smoke-clotted breath as she used the bed to keep herself upright. "Here!"

Logan appeared outside the window. His rough, disheveled face was the most beautiful thing she'd ever seen.

He climbed onto the HVAC unit below the window and reached for her, careful to avoid the jagged teeth of glass still protruding from the frame. "Come on! Let's go!"

She rose trembling to her feet, took a last staggering step, and then he was there, leaning through the shattered frame, lifting her up and pulling her out into the dazzling light, into the humid air bursting with precious oxygen, into bright, dizzying life.

Logan cradled her in his strong arms. He bounced and jostled her as he carried her across the lawn, but she didn't care.

She was safe. Safe from the flames and the suffocating smoke.

But Eden wasn't.

She wanted nothing more than to lay her head back, close her eyes, and give in to the lush, beguiling darkness sucking at the edges of her mind.

But she couldn't.

"Eden," she mumbled. "Find Eden."

She had to get down, had to go back in. She hadn't searched the walk-in closet or the master bathroom, hadn't braved the stairs to the second floor.

Eden could still be in there, scared and suffering and alone.

"Let me go!" Dakota shoved weakly at Logan's chest, trying to break free.

"Damn it, you crazy girl!" Logan only tightened his grip on her, cursing as the glass shards protruding from her palms scraped his arms. "Stop it!"

Desperation drove her. She squirmed harder, fighting him, fighting the darkness, fighting fate and chaos and everything that had conspired against her since the day she was born. "I need—I have to—"

"Stop! You aren't listening!"

She punched him as hard as she could right in his scruffy jaw.

Logan stumbled. He didn't drop her. He hissed a pained breath and crushed her against him, trapping her flailing hands even as she went for his eyeballs with her fingernails. "Hot damn. You're more trouble than you're worth, you know that?"

"Eden!" she wailed into his chest, struggling against him. She pounded his chest in futile despair.

The pain of loss was inside her like a heavy stone pressing down on her chest, breaking her into shards, into a hundred thousand pieces.

She had to go back in, even if it killed her. She'd fight to her last breath. She'd never give up. *Never, never.*

"Dakota! Listen to me!"

She heard his voice as if from far away, as if she were underwater and he were calling to her from somewhere up in the bright, bright sky.

"Eden is safe," Logan said. "She's right here."

41

DAKOTA

Dakota came to slowly, and then all at once.

She floated somewhere in pleasant darkness, in a comforting cocoon: a warm, pulsing womb she didn't want to leave, not ever.

Eden's safe. She's right here.

She jerked awake, gasping for air as if she'd just broken through the surface of a deep ocean.

"Careful!" Shay knelt over her, gently picking the last of the glass shards from her knees. "You suffered smoke inhalation and a few dozen small lacerations. I don't know how serious the smoke inhalation is, yet. Take it easy."

Dakota sat up fast, fighting the wooziness until her head cleared. For a moment, she couldn't remember who or where she was.

She wasn't in her apartment, lying on her cheap, saggy mattress with her lumpy pillow and rattling fan that couldn't make up for the crappy air conditioner.

She was outside. An ant crawled up her arm. Sharp blades of St. Augustine grass pricked her legs and butt.

She sat in a perfectly manicured yard. The grass was a vivid green, uniformly trimmed, completely free of weeds. In Miami, people paid good money for a yard like that, she thought dimly.

She stared down at her hands without recognizing them. They were wrapped in white gauze. Shay had bandaged them while she was unconscious.

She could feel Band-Aids stuck to her arms beneath her shirt-sleeves, which Shay had carefully rolled back down and re-duct-taped.

"Thank you," she rasped.

"You're welcome." Shay squeezed her shoulder. "How do you feel?"

"Awful." Her voice was hoarse, her throat raw. It felt like someone had scraped her airway with a knife.

It hurt to breathe. And her lungs still burned like she couldn't take in enough oxygen.

Because of the fire.

It all came back then. The nuclear explosion, the race to the theater, the attack in Old Navy, the arduous journey to find her sister.

"Eden—" She started to get up. A violent coughing fit wracked her body. Fresh pain speared through her fiercely aching head.

She sank back to the grass.

"What did I say about taking it easy?" Shay said sternly. "You need oxygen, a chest X-ray, complete blood cell count, a metabolic profile, and bedrest. I can't do anything about most of that until we get to the EOC, but you *must* rest, do you understand?"

Blearily, Dakota nodded. Her thoughts were still coming muddled and disjointed.

"Are you experiencing difficulty breathing?" Shay asked.

She shook her head. It hurt like hell, and it felt like her lungs would never get enough air again, but at least she could breathe.

"Prolonged coughing spells—"

In response, another coughing spasm gripped her.

"Okay, yes to that one. How about mental confusion? That's common with smoke inhalation injuries. You've already been hit on the head today."

"It's—it's coming back," she whispered huskily.

"Good, that's good." Shay sank back on her heels and touched her own head wound gingerly. "I didn't let anyone come near you until I'd checked you out. You gave us all a scare."

With a slow, careful movement, Dakota looked around, searching for her sister.

To the east, smoke poured into the sky. Flames licked at the windows of a dozen houses at the end of the street. Creaking, groaning sounds reached them, the dull roar of wood popping, things splintering, houses heaving, caving in on themselves, walls collapsing.

To the west, the sky was clear of smoke. The sun descended, the clouds striped with great scarves of color. The palm trees lining the street waved gently in the breeze.

The stately, stucco houses looked perfect but for their broken windows and the splinters of glass glinting in the manicured bushes. Shiny Audis, BMWs, and Mercedes dotted the driveways. Other than their group, not a person was in sight.

"Why she went through the back way is beyond me," Logan was saying. "Most normal people use the front door. She would've seen the kid sitting right there on the neighbor's lawn."

He leaned against the rear end of the apple-red Tesla parked in the brick driveway ten feet away, arms crossed over his chest. Julio stood beside him, eating a granola bar and peering down at her with concern in his dark eyes.

Park rested on the stretcher parked next to the curb at the end of the driveway. Harlow was bent over him, checking on his dressings.

"Are you sure you're okay?" Julio asked her.

Only one thought dominated Dakota's jumbled thoughts.

"Eden!" she rasped. "Where's Eden?"

And then the girl was there, running across the grass—short and plump, her long blonde hair streaming behind her, her beautiful face split in a huge grin.

Eden collapsed into Dakota's arms.

4 2

DAKOTA

Dakota wrapped her arms around her sister's soft, round body and squeezed as hard as she could. She barely felt the stinging cuts on her arms and hands, her throbbing head, her raw and burning throat.

She didn't care. She never wanted to let go.

They held each other, desperate and fierce and elated.

Waves of relief washed through her as she breathed in her sister's smoke-singed hair. She nestled her cheek against Eden's silken head and closed her eyes.

"I thought I'd lost you," she whispered hoarsely.

For the first time since the bomb exploded on TV, her chest expanded, the tightness releasing like a balloon sailing up, up, up into a brilliant blue sky.

It didn't matter how scorched her lungs felt, or how raw her throat was. She could breathe again.

Whatever was next, whatever was coming for them, she could handle it, as long as Eden was safe by her side. Once they got to Ezra's, they would both be safe. They'd finally be home.

Finally, she pulled back to examine her sister. Everything was there—the long, shiny golden-blonde curls, the bright blue eyes the color of cornflowers, the wide, generous mouth and freckles like nutmeg sprinkled across her chubby cheeks.

Eden was beautiful. So beautiful it made Dakota's heart hurt.

She clutched Eden's face between her bandaged hands. "I've got you. You're safe now. I'm here. I'm here, and I'm not leaving you again. Never, ever."

Even as she spoke the words, she knew they weren't entirely true.

The danger wasn't over. The sun was starting to set, the sky streaked with faint shades of red and orange and yellow. It was 7:19 p.m.

They'd been exposed to radiation for far longer than she'd planned. They felt fine now, but for how long?

They were all near the acute radiation sickness threshold, especially Eden, who'd been stuck in a flimsy house for over two days. She'd had the least protection of any of them.

They needed to get out of the hot zone, still a mile west, and then find shelter for the night. Then tomorrow, using the map, they'd trek through six miles of heavy suburbia to reach the EOC at Miami International.

Dakota, Shay, and Park would receive medical attention. Julio would head off to find his wife. Then Dakota, Eden, and whoever chose to come with them would continue on another fourteen miles or so, past Dolphin Mall, through Fontainebleau and Sweetwater, to the edge of the Everglades.

After that, it was another forty miles to the cabin.

It sounded easy enough—until she considered the power outages, the looting and rioting, the roaming gangs battling over fresh territory in a ruined ghost of a city without police or laws.

They'd killed a member of the Blood Outlaws. There would be consequences. She was certain of that.

And there was still the possible threat of Maddox to contend with, somewhere out there...

Tomorrow's troubles would come soon enough. She'd already suffered enough trouble today to last a lifetime.

Dakota forced herself to focus on the here and now, on her sister's dazzling smile.

In a minute, she'd rise and turn her thoughts to the journey ahead, but for this moment, this precious, glorious moment, she had everything she needed.

The End

SNEAK PEEK OF FROM THE ASHES

Dakota Sloane kissed her younger sister tenderly on the forehead. After the desperate journey through Miami to reach her, after nearly dying in the fire herself, Dakota never wanted to let Eden go.

Finally, she forced herself to pull away. She traced the girl's soft, beautiful features with her finger. "Are you sure you're okay?"

Eden fluttered her hands furiously, shaping them in ways Dakota recognized as sign language, but she didn't know their meaning.

"Use this." Dakota pulled Eden's notepad out from beneath her shirt and thrust it into Eden's moving hands. The cover was sweat-dampened, the edges of the paper curled from the heat. "What happened? Where were you?"

"She was with me," spoke a familiar voice.

Dakota stopped breathing.

"Eden, come here," the man commanded.

Before Dakota could react, Eden pulled free of her arms, leapt to her feet, and scurried out of reach.

Slowly, dread pooling in her gut, Dakota rose on trembling legs and turned around.

"You should sit back down, Dakota," Shay said, but Dakota heard her voice from some distant, far place. Everything faded away but for one thing.

The man stood several yards away, in the shade of a magnolia tree planted in the center of the manicured yard. He remained in the shadows, his hand slung loosely over the pistol at his hip.

An icy chill crept up her spine. She could hardly force any oxygen into her tortured lungs, her heart a fist in her throat.

No, no, no...

She'd made it so far, come so close...

"I saved her from that fire," the man said, mirth in his voice, as if there could possibly be anything to laugh about. "Good timing, wouldn't you say? Almost like a divine appointment."

"He said he's your brother." Logan Garcia glanced from Dakota's stricken face back to Eden, who nestled next to the man, happily gazing up at him with a delighted, earnest trust that twisted like a knife in Dakota's belly.

Of course, Eden trusted him. Because she didn't know.

Guilt skewered Dakota. She'd made the decision not to tell her the truth. Because she thought she knew better. Because she was trying to protect her sister the best she could.

And if she was completely honest with herself, it was because she couldn't bear the thought of Eden discovering what she'd done.

It had been so much easier to allow Eden to continue to trust her blindly, without the complications of what had happened that night stretching between them like an unbridgeable chasm.

Deep down, Dakota was terrified that Eden would never forgive her.

And now that choice had come back to bite them both in the ass.

"Maddox," Dakota whispered in a strangled voice.

The man stepped out from beneath the shadow of the tree, Eden at his side. He slung his left arm around Eden's shoulder, his right hand still resting carelessly on the butt of his gun.

Like he was just a friendly family man. Like his every move wasn't a threat.

She knew better.

He was always ready, always prepared. Just like she knew he would be.

His movements only appeared languid and casual. His shoulders were slightly hunched, his neck strained. Every fiber of his being strained with tension, a band about to snap.

At twenty-two years old, Maddox Cage had the grim, rough handsomeness of a man several years older. His face was long and angular with even features and dirty-blonde hair shorn close to his skull.

He was lean and rangy like a stray dog—tough, powerful, and dangerous.

She hadn't seen him other than a few glimpses in three years, but he remained exactly as he was in her memories and her nightmares.

Only, his pallor was tinged a sickly, unhealthy yellow, his lips dry and cracked, his sharp blue eyes glassy with fever.

He'd been exposed to radiation.

How much, she didn't know. Not enough to kill him or slow him down, not yet anyway. He still looked as strong as he ever had.

Shay clapped her hands, delighted. "Oh, a family reunion! How wonderful!"

Maddox grinned at her with a flash of white teeth. "It's some kind of reunion, isn't it, Dakota?"

Dakota's fingers twitched, desperate to go for the Sig, but Eden was right there in the line of fire.

In the time it would take to draw her weapon, Maddox could do whatever he wanted to Eden. Put a gun to her head. Slit her throat.

Dakota knew better than to discount any possibility.

She couldn't do a thing, and Maddox knew it.

"It's good to see you, Dakota. I can't tell you how much I've missed you." His words sounded real, his smile genuine. It even lit up those glassy blue eyes, drawing her in with its disarming warmth.

She was never quite sure whether it was a ruse or if he truly believed in his own goodness. He was a trickster, a god of mischief and destruction, of many faces: at turns kind, indifferent, cruel.

He kept you off-balance. Using your own weaknesses against you. Twisting tenderness and affection into weapons wielded to control, to dominate.

But Dakota wasn't a scared, timid sixteen-year-old anymore. She knew better now. She knew what he wanted, what he'd come for.

A hundred yards behind them, the raging fire consumed house after house, hissing and crackling. The sun sank slowly toward the horizon, twilight hovering at the edges of the sky.

The breeze cooled her hot skin. Somewhere, a bird burst into song.

She could still fix this. She had to fix it.

Her stinging, bandaged hand inched toward the butt of her gun.

"You shouldn't be here," she said hoarsely, in barely above a whisper. "You don't belong here."

"I have a right to be here more than you do," he said, still smiling. He licked his cracked lips. "We both know that."

She swayed on her feet, dizzy from the lack of oxygen, from whatever damage the smoke inhalation had done to her lungs. She coughed and cleared her throat. "Eden, get away from him. Right now."

Confused, Eden gestured something that Dakota couldn't understand. She remained at Maddox's side.

"Easy now, Dakota," he said smoothly. "I think the smoke inhalation did something to your head. It causes confusion and mental changes, doesn't it? You know me. We're *family*, right?"

Maddox's gaze shot to the holster at her hip, her fingers creeping toward the butt of the Sig. His eyes sharpening, glittering like a predator's.

He gave the smallest shake of his head. *Don't even try it.*

Defeated, she lowered her hand, helpless anger and fear slashing through her.

Another coughing fit gripped her. When she could breath again, she glared at him. "You're nothing to me," she spat.

Logan was up off the fender of the Tesla now, tense and alert. He hadn't reached for his own weapon yet, but he looked ready to if needed.

Shay and Julio stared at Dakota, too startled by this sudden turn of events to even say anything. At the curb, Harlow and Park watched silently, their expressions perplexed.

No one understood what was really happening here.

"Dakota, what's going on?" Logan asked.

"I can explain," she said, her voice cracking, panic creeping in.

"Why don't I give it a try?" Maddox tightened his hold on Eden's shoulder. "I'm sure I can explain everything just fine."

"No," she whispered. "You can't."

Maddox smiled at her, sharp as a blade.

His pale skin and sunken eyes gave him almost a gaunt, ghoulish appearance. Even sick, he still had that keen-edged hunger in his gaze.

He was the kind of man who was never satisfied, who always craved what he didn't have, who always wanted more.

All the old terrors she'd worked so hard to defeat came roaring back, stronger than ever.

A tremor went through her body, like she was standing too close to the edge of a cliff, about to fall. Her bones vibrated beneath her skin. Her heart shuddered inside her chest.

She felt every brand on her back, scorched and seared and throbbing—like the moment she'd received each one at Maddox's hand.

And his words, hissed in her ear: *For the Lord shall execute judgment by fire...You deserve far worse, you know that, don't you? But I am merciful, because I love you...*

She swallowed the acid burning the back of her raw, singed throat. Her knees trembled, but she forced herself to remain standing. "You need to leave. Just turn and go, right now."

Maddox turned to the others. "My name is Maddox Cage. And I am *Eden's* brother."

"Eden's—?" Logan's bewildered gaze flicked from Eden to Dakota to Maddox.

"She told you they were sisters, didn't she?"

"We are!" Dakota croaked.

"She's a liar, too," he said with relish. "And a thief. An interloper. An intruder."

"No," she said weakly. "No—"

"Dakota Sloane is no sister of Eden's," Maddox said triumphantly, his lip curling. "Dakota is her kidnapper."

To be continued...

AUTHOR'S NOTE

I hope you enjoyed *Fear the Fallout*! While I tried to be accurate with the setting of Miami, some names and places were adjusted for the sake of the story.

As I researched improvised nuclear devices and their potential for destruction, I found some competing information.

The reality is, we don't know exactly what a nuclear ground-burst detonation in a modern urban city would look like.

Hopefully, we never have to find out.

That being said, I tried to be accurate with the nuclear information I included while also being true to the story and the characters.

Thank you so much for reading.

ACKNOWLEDGMENTS

Thank you as always to my awesome beta readers. Your thoughtful critiques and enthusiasm are invaluable.

Thank you Becca and Brendan Cross, Lauren Nikkel, Michelle Browne, Jessica Burland, Sally Shupe, Janice Love, Jordyn McGinnity, Jeremy Steinkraus, and Barry and Derise Marden.

To Michelle Browne for her skills as a great developmental and line editor. Thank you to Eliza Enriquez for her excellent proofreading skills. You both make my words shine.

And a special thank you to Jenny Avery for volunteering her time to give the manuscript that one last read-through and catch any stray errors. Any remaining errors are mine.

To my husband, who takes care of the house, the kids, and the cooking when I'm under the gun with a writing deadline.

And to my kids, who show me the true meaning of love every day and continually inspire me. I love you.

ABOUT THE AUTHOR

I spend my days writing apocalyptic and dystopian fiction novels. I love writing stories exploring how ordinary people cope with extraordinary circumstances, especially situations where the normal comforts, conveniences, and rules are stripped away.

My favorite stories to read and write deal with characters struggling with inner demons who learn to face and overcome their fears, launching their transformation into the strong, brave warrior they were meant to become.

Some of my favorite books include *The Road*, *The Passage*, *Hunger Games*, and *Ready Player One*. My favorite movies are *The Lord of the Rings* and *Gladiator*.

Give me a good story in any form and I'm happy.

I love to hear from my readers! Find my books and chat with me via any of the channels below:

www.Facebook.com/KylaStoneAuthor

www.Amazon.com/author/KylaStone

Email me at KylaStone@yahoo.com

Made in United States
North Haven, CT
18 December 2024